FORESEEN

Christina Casino

First Edition, September 2022

Originally published by Christina Casino, Greensburg.

Cover art design © copyright by Christina Casino

Printed in the United States of America

Visit https://www.christinacasino.com

Library of Congress Control Number: 2022914724

ISBN 979-8-218-04936-2 (pb)

ISBN 979-8-218-04937-9 (e-book)

"And with the click of a button, I did something
I never did before…I took a chance."
Christina Casino

Table of Contents

Chapter I

Free Ride

The only item I kept from the mansion was an old dictionary that had been passed down from generation to generation – given to each first son of the family. I read the definition of the word that I was currently exhibiting – silently to myself – while sitting in the only diner that was reasonably close to our home before the road stretched on to nowhere for miles and miles.

The word *freedom* by definition means the power or right to act, speak, or think as one wants without hindrance or restraint. I ran my fingers over the word and its definition as if it were written in braille on the pages before me. While doing so, I closed my eyes and breathed lightly.

Freedom, the feeling of it, the smell of it – like nothing I could describe. Nothing anyone could take from me now. From this day forward I would fight for my freedom. I would kill for it if I had to. I did kill for it because I had to.

My situation gave me no choice. *Wrong.* My situation did give me a choice and so I chose. I chose to kill because it was what was right for me. I did this for me. No one else would have. I have to

1

always look out for myself from now on because there is no one left to take care of me, but me.

"Will that be all for you today?" a young pregnant lady asked sweetly as she slowly rubbed her protruding belly. For a moment I had fallen so deep into thought I had forgotten where I was and what it was that I was doing until she yanked me back to reality.

"Yes, please I'll just take the bill and be on my way," I said, although in my mind I was hesitating about moving from this very spot.

There was just one other word that I wanted to physically read the definition of. Licking my fingertip, I frantically flipped the pages until I got to the k section of the dictionary. It was a word that had me curious as to how bad it could get.

Karma. A person's previous actions result in the fate of his or her future. I'd like to think karma and I already crossed paths many times throughout my life. But then again it always seemed to have a way of sneaking up on me when I least expected it to visit.

Like an ugly step-sister, she appeared at the most inconvenient moments. But I knew I would have to take whatever punishment came my way once the two of us reunited. There was nothing I could do about the subject. Certain actions warrant certain consequences and that was a lesson I had seen and learned time and time again.

The waitress was back promptly with the check in hand and a genuine smile on her face. I gave her more than enough to cover the bill and told her to keep the rest for her tip. I could tell she needed the money. She looked as if she could go into labor any day and I wanted to help her if I could.

I would've wanted someone to help me and my baby if we needed it. I wondered to myself silently if I would've looked like her. Would my belly have been that large and noticeable? Would I have rubbed it out of habit too? Would I have talked to it throughout the day when I was lonely and sang to it at night before bed? There were so many things that could've been – that should've been but they just weren't meant to be. I forced myself to swallow the knot that had moved from my chest and made its way into the back of my throat. This was no time for emotions to be getting the best of me.

The woman thanked me repeatedly and I assured her it was my pleasure. Remembering the time my father tipped Danny more than enough to cover the bill on our visit to the café – that first time I ever saw him. In a saddened manner I sighed to myself not only for the particular memory but for his memory in general creeping into my thoughts.

3

Once she was gone, I took a moment to rub my invisible belly and what once slept in there. I would always remember my child; it would forever haunt my dreams not knowing if it had been a girl or a boy.

"Excuse me, I'm sorry to interrupt but are you the woman in need of a ride? One of the waitresses by the kitchen mentioned that they thought you were the one who asked about it." The confused man hovered over me like a tree casting a shadow on the grass below. He removed his hat just once, using it to scratch the remaining hair on the top of his head.

"Yes, that is me – I'm Abriana," I said with an extended hand and a sincere smile.

Reaching his to meet mine, we shook with a hard grip that came from both of us. Along with that, he shared with me a smile that met his eyes as he said, "Good to meet you, the names Travis. Well, they just called out my to-go meal so as soon as I grab that I am getting ready to hit the road if you'd like to get a move on."

"I am ready to get going when you are Travis."

"Great! Let's head out then!" he said in a chipper tone starting his stroll towards his to-go meal. Travis was an elderly man who walked with a slight gimp though he tried his best not to show it.

He stood an easy six or seven feet tall with broad shoulders and a large belly that protruded out from his pants. Strapped tightly around him were a pair of old overalls clipped to the top of his bottoms. The hair sticking out of his hat was as white as a cotton ball and was braided – allowing the length of it to hang just between his shoulder blades. A wrinkled and quite dirty handkerchief peeked out from the pocket of his shirt being held tightly in place tucked behind one of his overall straps.

Once we had started on our way Travis kept up with our little chat, mainly filled with questions. I was relieved to have a conversation since it would have been awkward if we rode in silence, but at the same time, I felt uneasy about being asked some things that I may not want to give answers to.

"So, the kitchen tells me you're a hitchhiker…" The look on my face must have told him I was less than pleased with the comment since he paused for a brief moment before continuing. "Sorry, it's a uh– small diner. Everybody knows everybody's business in that place. Whether you come in regularly or you are just passing through, you can't help but be the subject of discussion."

"I see…" I said a little annoyed between my clenched teeth. "I guess I can see where someone might get the idea of me being a hitchhiker. The only thing that doesn't add up is that I have no bags or belongings with me. Usually, a hitchhiker has some sort of survival items for their travels don't you think?" I gave a small smirk in his direction to let him know I wasn't offended by his comments or the thoughts of others. Little did he know if I was someone who had such soft skin, I would've never been able to make it through half the things I had been through.

"Well, you got that old book holding tight to you. That's a belonging if you ask me," he said, tipping his head towards it as he observed the look on my face while we drove on.

"True but this wouldn't do anything in terms of survival out here to help me along in my journeys…if you ask me," I said repeating his last line – my small smirk turning into a slight smile of amusement. In my mind, I waited for him to question why I was even carrying it on my person if it wasn't any help to me, but that statement never came.

Catching on and hearing my purposeful repetition he laughed a jingle that sounded like Christmas itself. It's what I pictured Santa's laugh being like – jolly and carefree. I couldn't help but grin even more at him, his rosy cheeks and nose were glistening with sweat in the daylight. And when he laughed it was infectious and hard not to smile in his presence. He seemed like a ball full of happiness and it was the type of energy I needed to be around, especially right now.

He lifted his hat off just enough to use the rim of it to scratch his itchy head as he had done once before. "I get it. I get it – you don't want to be questioned and that's okay. I am still trying to figure out why for the life of me someone would just drop you off in the middle of nowhere like that and leave you stranded. That's all."

"No one dropped me off, Travis. I walked to the diner – all by myself like a big girl."

Letting out a whistle he shook his head like a disapproving father would which was then followed swiftly by a hard chuckle. "My, my – you sure are a loaded gun, Miss Abriana."

Travis, you have no idea. "Why thank you, I'll take that as the first compliment you've paid me so far today." I continued laughing hard at his loaded gun comment well after he had said it.

"How come nobody could drop you off? They too scared of you?" he asked. "Too afraid that you're going to shoot them!" He let out a small chuckle that could've gone unnoticed had I not been paying attention.

"Are you *mocking* me, sir?" I asked him turning my body halfway to look at him.

"No ma'am, I most certainly am not! I wouldn't do that to a lady! Back in the day, our mama's raised their men right. Not these boys in this day and age." The wrinkles around his eyes quickly vanished as his mood switched from happy to serious. Pulling the handkerchief from his pocket he lightly patted the part of his forehead that was showing just under the brim of his hat before quickly wiping it down over his face and neck.

Before Travis could get his handkerchief back in his pocket the car began to veer off the road as it continued to gain speed. Glancing over at him I saw that he was clenching his chest hard with one hand while the other remained white-knuckled on the steering wheel. His face was bright red and held a look of horror. At this point he wasn't even looking at the road anymore – he was staring straight up at the roof of the car in a trance-like state – huffing, puffing, and wheezing out what small breaths he could.

"OH TRAVIS!" I cried out as his hand dropped from the wheel entirely. Grabbing it quickly to steer, I tried my best to keep the car on the road as we winded down the mountain side. Travis had completely passed out in the driver's side seat and foam had begun to drizzle from his mouth. All I wanted to do was cry and panic at the same time. But I knew crying would only lead me to not see what was ahead of us and panicking would leave me to rash decision-making – possibly harming us both.

As the road curved tighter and tighter with each downward turn I began to think about what else I could do when the lightbulb in my head went off. Slow the car down – hit the brakes! The only problem was Travis's foot was lodged on the gas pedal and he weighed at least three hundred pounds there was no way I would be able to move it. Now I understand why Gabriel said driving could be a dangerous act. I was living this nightmare out while I was wide awake. Was this karma coming to get me already? Was it right now – this instant – that I would be faced with the consequences for all I had done wrong?

I only remember a few images. The first was how fast the tree was coming at us or rather how fast we were coming at the tree. Then me flying out of the windshield in a petrified state, hearing what sounded like the snapping of bones and knowing that I will surely die. After all, I had done this would be my end. This was meant to be my fate. My karma. My death. They would never find my body because no one was looking for me. I would watch from above as my body decayed and the seasons covered my skin until it fell away from my bones leaving only a separated skeleton. The final image – I caught while my body was being flipped in the air – was catching a fragment of the car bend around the tree before tumbling down over the mountain's unforgiving cliff – taking both Travis and the tree down with it.

Chapter II

Investigation

A smell so familiar wound its way up my nostrils. It was the smell of strands of life accompanied by near-death experiences.

"Welcome back," a nurse's voice greeted me warmly as my eyes struggled not to flutter while they opened.

Coincidentally when I regained full consciousness, I found it to be the twin of the nurse that had first welcomed me back to life when I had the miscarriage

"Do you have a twin sister?" I asked her groggily. "Or…if you're not a twin, did you used to work in a different hospital?"

To that, she began to laugh just as her cheeks blushed the lightest shade of pink. "I am glad to see you have a sense of humor Miss. You will certainly be needing that during your time rehabilitating. But alas I have no sister, I am an only child and this has been the only hospital I have ever had the pleasure of working in." She continued to smile warmly at me as she wrote down some notes on the pages she held. "Now – tell me, do you know what your name is?"

Before I could answer her, two men in police uniforms entered the room interrupting our conversation. The first was a tall man with a large build and big hands while the second was much shorter than him with a more proportioned body.

"Excuse me, we apologize for the interruption but we heard the patient was awake now and we've been waiting a long time to speak with her."

"Well excuse me for saying so!" the nurse said in an outrage. "But I don't think she is in any state right now to discuss her accident. I mean – for heaven's sake the poor girl just woke up! Give her a chance to breathe and allow us to fill in the gaps."

"That protocol is incorrect we need *her* to fill in the gaps for *us*, not the other way around," the larger police man argued as his irritation began to show. "Ma'am we know you are just doing your job but we must ask you to kindly step outside while we talk with the young lady.

"I want to see your badges! There have been the same two men here all week and I have *never* seen you two before. Show me your forms of identification immediately!"

The first man was not taking no for an answer. Nor did he budge to present her with the badge she was asking for. His hands simply began to ball up with frustration when the nurse continued arguing with him instead of just leaving as he asked. "That won't be necessary ma'am. We are just the relieving police officers for the two that have been on duty all week."

"This is *ridiculous!* I am getting my supervisor!" the nurse told him as she stormed out of the room putting her finger in his face as she pointed at him.

"Sorry, you feel that way, ma'am. We got a job to do too and we are just trying to do it." His voice spoke louder and louder to keep up with her pace so that his final words might reach her before the door closed behind her.

After the nurse bolted from the room. I watched as the larger man signaled something to the smaller man with a head nod. In the blink of an eye, the shorter man hurried towards the door pushing it shut the rest of the way and locking it behind him.

"Now – now ma'am we know you've been through a lot but it's going to be very important that you try and remember every detail you can about what happened," the smaller police man said to me.

Eyeing him suspiciously I stuttered through my next statement. "Wh–why did you lock…the door behind you?"

"That way we don't be uh– *interrupted* would be the word I am looking for. Isn't that right

Antonio?" The smaller man looked to the taller one for some kind of support that I didn't quite understand.

"Yes Matteo," the taller man said, shaking his head just enough times to make himself believe the statement.

The nurse's words lingered in my head, ringing through my brain like a train whistle. Something about these two men just didn't seem right and I was starting to catch on to what the nurse had been going on about. Their body language and routine seemed incorrect for an officer. And refusing to show their badges seemed like a very odd thing to do. I would hardly call that proper protocol.

"Let's just start at the beginning. What do you say about that?" Antonio asked. "Matteo! Pull a chair over here for both of us! You can sit by one side of the bed and I'll sit by the other!" He pointed to the far side of the room closest to the window to be Matteo's seat while he motioned for him to be on the side by the door.

"The beginning…" I repeated. Not being entirely sure of where the beginning was at the moment.

"I'll start it off!" Antonio declared as his stiff body sat down hard on the chair, making it squeak under his shifting weight. "You were in a coma, right?"

"I was?" I asked uncertainly. "This is news to me…"

"Oh, gee! Would you look at that? Now the poor girl doesn't even know she just woke up from a coma Matteo!"

"Yes, yes, I heard Antonio. I'm right here." The change in Matteo's voice sounded like he was beginning to get frustrated already – and whether it was with me or his friend remained unknown.

"Can I see your badge?" I asked looking between the two of them while I spoke.

"May," Matteo said in return. "It's *may* I see your badge. Use your manners when you speak. I'm sure your parents taught you better than that!" With this, he erupted into a disturbing laugh, the kind that made me feel uneasy and covered my skin in goosebumps.

I could hear the sirens ringing in my head, drowning out my thoughts. And the *parent's comment* didn't sit well with me. Especially because of the way he said it – almost matter-of-factly – like he knew that my parents had taught me better. Chills ran up my spine as I tried to reassure myself that it was just a coincidence and nothing more.

"*May* I see *your badge?*" I said with equal frustration.

"You are in *no* position to be asking the questions here lady. Leave that part to us!" Antonio said with a smoker's cough that left him practically choking up a lung before spitting in a pan near my bed.

"You are exactly right about that!" Matteo agreed. "What you *can* see are the blank pages that I'm going to take notes on." He waved the pages practically in my face as Antonio chuckled some more. "Anyway, let's begin, shall we? Now what we *do* know is you were at a diner having some breakfast before hitching a ride with a man who was heading out of town. Is that correct so far or do you not remember any of that?"

"Why…yes that sounds about right," I said as I rubbed the top of my head softly. "I was having breakfast and I told my waitress that I was heading out of town–"

"I see," Matteo interrupted. "And just why were you heading out of town?"

"Would you let the girl speak on her *own*, Matteo!" Antonio yelled over at him.

"I–don't remember," I lied while trying my best to look him straight in the eye so that he didn't think anything was out of the ordinary.

16

"Continue please," Antonio coaxed me to finish telling them what I remember.

I was pushing on my temples hoping that it would help to clear up some of the fog I was experiencing but even still, I could only see bits and pieces. "The waitress told me that there was a man seated near the front of the diner who was waiting on a to-go order and that he was a familiar customer who was just passing through. She thought that maybe he could give me a ride and offered to ask him for me. To which I agreed. Then he and I exchanged words and we left."

"Now what do you mean by *exchanged words?*" Matteo asked, attempting to dig deeper into something that wasn't there.

"We were agreeing on the transportation…" I answered confusingly. Either he wasn't following what I was saying or I wasn't making any sense when I spoke.

"Uh-huh. And what happened after that?" he asked while continuing to quickly scribble down notes as I spoke.

"Then…we were driving…" I said trailing off in thought as my memories got more and more blurry.

"And what happened while you were driving?" Matteo pushed, tapping his writing utensil on his lap impatiently.

"I–uhh…" I couldn't remember. Just like that, there was nothing but a blank space. Like nothing had happened after we left the diner.

"You were driving down a windy road." Antonio tried to help jump-start my memories back as he wound his hand in a circular motion as if to hurry me along but it didn't seem to work like that.

"I'm sorry. I'm afraid I can't remember right now. Nothing about the drive is coming back to me at the present moment," I said to them sincerely.

"Alright well we will get there," Antonio said almost kindly.

"So, tell us," Matteo started once more. "Where were you before the diner?"

"Be–*before* the diner…" I couldn't help but stutter and choke on the words coming out of my mouth because that part I could remember quite clearly. It was the whole reason why I was there. Why and how I ended up at the diner. This can't be happening. I tried to think to myself what to say and how to act to not look suspicious in any way. I had to remind myself to *stay* calm.

"Yes, before the diner. Where were you? Where did you come from? I mean you had to come from somewhere, right? Besides your mothers ah–" Antonio's smoker cough interrupted the sentence before it could be finished and I was quite thankful for that since I knew the crude manner in which that was going. But Matteo only laughed at the absurdity of the questions he was asking me, winking at Antonio in a distasteful way. *Scum.*

"Well...I was...umm–" I tried to think quickly on my feet to come up with something to tell them but nothing was coming to mind.

Lucky for me a knock came at the door once it failed to open normally with the force of a push, which then was followed by loud, repetitive pounding. "Open this door immediately!" the nurse yelled from the other side as she began to jiggle the door handle.

"Who dropped you off?" Matteo continued, ignoring the nurse's request.

"Drop– me off?" This was a nightmare. A living nightmare. Did they know something else? Were they here for something else?

The nurse continued banging on the door – tugging hard at the door handle that refused to budge. The constant sounds threw off my concentration completely. But I wasn't surprised since I felt scatterbrained ever since I opened my eyes. I could hear another voice with her – which I assumed was her superior that she went to get – telling her to go and get the spare set of keys from the desk drawer.

I could tell by Matteo's face that he was less than pleased to have to repeat the question. "That's what I asked. *Who* dropped you off at the diner?"

I decided maybe it would be easier if I looked at Antonio this time when I answered instead of Matteo. Maybe that would make it easier for me to come up with an answer if I wasn't staring at the person who was writing everything I said down. "No one did. I hitchhiked there. I'm a hitchhiker." Deciding to go with that as an answer to his question since for some reason the word *hitchhiker* was ringing through my thoughts.

To this Antonio busted out laughing – throwing his head back with such force I was sure his neck would snap. "You are not a *damn* hitchhiker! You are a comedian though! Unless you think we are stupid?"

I had to convince them that I was. I just had to. "I *really* am a hitchhiker! Ask the waitress I had at the diner or some of the other employees working there if you don't believe me! And I bet they'll tell you the same thing!"

"You don't have any equipment! How do you expect to survive out there without...well, without anything!" Antonio busted out laughing yet again.

This time I attempted to speak a little louder with a harsher tone so that they would begin to take me seriously. "I must have lost my equipment during my uh– black out or else I'd show you."

"Well now, that there is really interesting. Now isn't it, Antonio? You see when we questioned the people at the diner, they did say they saw you walking which that part checks out alright but when I asked them if they thought that maybe you were a hitchhiker, they told me no because you had nothing with you but a book. A dictionary to be more specific is I think what the pregnant lady said. Hold on now let me flip back through my notes." Matteo licked the tips of his fingers to flip back through his pages to ensure he had repeated the statement accurately.

A loud bang came from the opposite side of the room from where we were sitting, making everyone turn to see what all the fuss was about. "YOU TWO! Get the *hell* out of this patient's room now!" my nurse practically screamed at the top of her lungs. Her face was beat red and her hands were flailing about everywhere as she spoke.

"Now, now! That's no way to talk to an officer Ma'am." Matteo said in a gratified way pulling out a toothpick to chew on.

"I called down to the station. And the two officers on duty are running late due to another emergency! Now I don't know who the *hell* you two are but you better get out of this hospital before I have you *thrown* out by security!"

Matteo stared back at his partner with a humorously nasty grin spread across his face. "I didn't know we were going to have to do this the hard way. Did you Antonio?"

Antonio simply laughed his goofy laugh in response and then stopped abruptly. "For your information Ma'am we are the law around here. And it'll do you well to remember that!" Antonio's tone was quite aggressive with every word he spoke. It almost seemed like he was more the muscle behind the two while Matteo was the interrogator. He then got up and stormed out of the room being sure to stare down the nurse and her superior on the way out.

Matteo bent down to collect his jacket from the chair before making eye contact with me. "This won't be the last time you'll be seeing us. We will be back when you are feeling better and your memories start to come back." He turned from me and tipped his hat at the two ladies on the way out the door. "Oh, and by the way, I almost forgot...you didn't happen to see a house fire while you were hitchhiking, did you? It was from the direction you were seen coming from and you couldn't have possibly missed the smoke. It was a mile high."

"No, I'm afraid I don't recall noticing, sorry. I tend to stare down at my feet when I walk," I said, gulping down the vomit that was burning in the back of my throat.

He chuckled slightly, looking between the other two women before looking back at me. "Well now that's also interesting – that doesn't sound like a trait an experienced hitchhiker would do. Normally you'll have your eyes on the road ahead of you to signal someone traveling in your direction." He paused momentarily – pulling the toothpick completely from his mouth – probably to see if I had anything else to say on the matter which I did not. "Alright well, that's all I got for you for now. And it's not a big deal about the house fire. Some men just died while it was burning down and we are investigating it. My partner seems to think someone had something to do with it. That someone purposefully started the blaze. The whole house went up in flames – just completely engulfed it. Creepy!" He mockingly shivered before stepping out into the hallway and eventually strolling away. "You ladies have a nice day now."

Chapter III

Rehabilitation

The following day my nurse and her assistant were in my room early in the morning – throwing open the windows to let the rising sun shine on my face.

"Good morning! We weren't properly introduced yesterday with all the shenanigans. My name is Carly and I'll be your nurse. I've been the one primarily taking care of you since you came in. And this here is my assistant Jenny, she's learning the trade."

Jenny gave me a small smile as she opened up the feet rest of a wheelchair that she had pushed over while Carly was introducing herself.

"Hello. It's nice to meet you both. But uh– if I may ask...why the early morning rise and shine?"

Jenny began to giggle as did Carly. "Didn't I tell you she is a hoot!" Carly seemed so proud of this particular trait that I held. "Well dear, we are going to wheel you down to physical therapy to start the rehabilitation process."

"Rehabila– what?" My attempt to repeat the word had failed me.

They giggled once more before Carly started explaining it to me further. "Oh, you are a sweetheart aren't you! So, to put it not in medical terms – you simply broke some bones during your accident. The injuries you sustained were repaired by the doctor – to the best of his abilities – when you first arrived here. We need to get your body up and moving again before those bones and muscles start to stiffen up and then we really have problems!" *That's comforting to hear, that I simply broke some bones and the doctor repaired them to the best of his abilities.* The words themselves made me queasy.

My eyes must have been bugging out of my head because Jenny stepped in to do some reassuring. "It's going to be okay. I'm going to be with you during physical therapy – the whole time. I won't leave your side. You, me, and the others are all going to do it together. We are just going to take baby steps. There is *nothing* to worry about."

Although Jenny was practically a child herself, she had a soothing voice and a calmness in her words. If my baby would've been a girl, I would've hoped she grew up to be as caring and gentle as Jenny. And even though I was terrified inside it made me feel a little better knowing that I wouldn't be left alone with people I didn't know.

"Okay now you're going to feel some pain while we lift you to get you into the wheelchair," Carly explained. "Ready – one, two, three!"

Fast Forward:

After six months of rehabilitation, my hand and wrist movements were pretty much back to normal and after a year of rehabilitation, I was walking around almost as normal as before.

They had done several surgeries on me when I first arrived to save me and get me back to a stable condition. The rumor around the hospital was that I had lost so much blood and had sustained such horrific injuries they didn't think I was going to make it. But they tried their best to save my life anyway.

I didn't ask nor did I care to know what all they had done to me. The two most important surgeries that had to be done to me, I knew about and in my opinion, they were the only ones that mattered. The doctor tried to tell me what they all were but I plugged my ears and made loud noises. Letting him know that I just didn't want to know. I was not ready to know. It gave me the chills when he started describing them all and when nausea began to surface – that was it for me.

I didn't dare ask what they had done to make my body parts work again. I was just thankful that they did. On more than one occasion my attractive doctor reminded me of just how lucky I was – to not only survive my accident but to live through the major surgeries and come out fairly normal.

I did not see the two men who had been there to question me the first day I came out of my coma. They simply disappeared and never came back. Which was a blessing in disguise for me. Obviously, something I had said was enough for them to not have to return. In realizing that, relief fell over me even though the whole time I stayed in the hospital I remained anxious. I was practically living on edge that they were just going to show up one random day and come walking through the door as they had done once before.

Within a matter of weeks, I had regained my memory of the accident. Everything from the diner, to the crash, and everything in between. In my dreams, I would re-live it – over and over again. Every night I would wake up screaming and my night shift nurse would come running in to calm me down, washing my face and neck with cold water to clean off the sweat.

After the first week of this happening, they had me start seeing a counselor in the hospital. They thought that maybe by talking about it would help get it out of my system enough to not re-live it every night in my dreams. It was a long time – months in fact – until I stopped having that dream.

The first thing I did when I initially left the hospital was, I went and visited the spot where the accident happened to place flowers there for Travis. Someone had put a large cross in the ground where the tree once stood. Travis's name was carved into it with the date he was born and the date of his accident. He was sixty-eight years old. There were no personal belongings or gifts from any others except a cross necklace that I noticed was hanging from his rear-view mirror when I first took my seat inside his vehicle. But it was then that I wondered if he even had any family at all.

Jenny had gone and done some research on her own about him and found out that his wife had died a long time ago from an illness that was unknown in the medical field. She was a baroness from England who had run away from her duties, home, and family just to be with her one true love who happened to be a peasant. Supposedly Travis spent time in England when he was a young man working for her family at their manor and that was how he met his wife.

The two knew her family would never let them be together since she was betrothed to marry one of the princes. Her runoff was quite the scandal and left both families not only disappointed but ashamed. Similarly, she had also been disowned and to that, I could relate and respect her. We learned that after her passing he had lived without her for over thirty years. She also learned that they had two children. A little girl who had died at childbirth and the other – a little boy – passed away suddenly during a terrible accident on their farm when he was just five years old. Their love story began like that out of a fairytale book but little did they know that they had been doomed from the start and their life would have more than one turn for the worst.

Ever since the loss of his wife, he went on the road, doing a delivery here and there for some side money but mostly he was running from the ghosts of his past that were always trying to catch up to him. The open road was like freedom for him too I suppose. It sounded to me that he thought if he kept on the move, it would prohibit him from dwelling on it all and slipping into sadness, falling victim to the drink…or worse.

At this moment I was thankful that he was able to be reunited with her and the kids after all these years. Their family could finally be together as one just as it always should've been. In the back of my mind, I just hoped that he didn't feel any pain during the accident. I just hoped that it was quick – done and over with before he even knew anything had happened.

I knelt in front of the cross and said a silent prayer before apologizing to him afterward. I felt like it was my fault. Maybe if we hadn't left in a rush we would've still been in the diner or sitting in the parking lot when it happened and we could've got him help. Maybe he'd still be here.

I was always told you can't blame yourself for the death of others because when it's their time to go, it's their time to go and there is nothing any of us can do to stop it or change it. That was his destiny. We all have a time, a date, and a place – you just never know when or where that is. In no book does it say that tomorrow is promised to you – if you wake up the next day that's a gift. It's because God allowed you to. Not because you are owed that day.

Chapter IV

Familiarity

Here I stood – allowing myself to get sucked into the thoughts that consumed my mind. But one thing was for sure – I never knew that watching the mansion burn down would bring me such relief, such a sense of peace. Not only that – it filled me with feelings I didn't even know I needed to experience or rather re-experience. The size of the flames, the intensity of the heat, and the smell in the air – all the things that made me so present in that moment. Something you can't turn away from because it will *not* be ignored.

"Are you alright?" Benson croaked from behind, interrupting me from blankly staring out the window as I replayed the memory of that day in my head.

"Yes, Benson. I am okay." The breath caught in my throat making for a weird tone as I tried to hide my feelings and cover the truth – all while answering as a proper widow would.

With an exaggerated huff, he said, "Okay well then stop breathing up the glass! You're practically fogging the whole window over there and customers are trying to look in!"

Rolling my eyes, I snorted silently so that he didn't hear me and scold me for that too. For an instant, it made me smile inside and out – to see how passionate he was now in general. Not only about his behavior but even more so about his bookstore and his customer's interactions. No matter his new disposition he was still the same old Benson to me. And he probably always would be.

He was real with me – not that he was fake with others – he was genuine with them but he was never afraid to put his finger in my face and tell me when I had done wrong. Or shoving unasked advice down my throat. For all these things and more I would always be grateful for him. I remember when I first came back, I had more guts than I ever had before. One day out of nowhere out came the courage to ask him if I could call him *Pap* since we had grown fonder of each other through the years. I'll never forget the look of death he gave me. It was that day I learned I will never ask that question again.

Making my way back to restocking the shelves in the back I tried to convince myself that I had done right by taking Gabriele's or rather Nicholas's advice – in not returning to the Greco's restaurant. Although he was gone that didn't mean I wasn't involved anymore. That any target that had been placed on him was removed from me. There was no get-out-of-free card in this dangerous lifestyle we lived, in the dangerous way we loved the ones we fell in love with. There was no out without permanently being removed – by death and only death.

I had made the decision to not allow myself to be chased off from here, running back to the sanctuary of Italy. I can still feel that hole that remained unfilled even when I was over there with relatives surrounding me and I knew it would still be the same. With no real family left here and the only people I knew were either Benson or the Greco's. I decided that the safer of the two was Benson. They knew where I worked before – sure. But maybe they didn't know about my precious bookstore and my rowdy Benson. Maybe they didn't have eyes on me all the time – following me here as well. *Wishful thinking,* a girl could still hope though. Hope was all she had, all this girl has at least.

Benson had been kind enough to let me work at the bookstore with him now, especially since business had really picked up. But he was sure to make me take an abundance of time off when I came back to the city with everything that had happened. Since I was *supposed* to be in mourning it sounded like the appropriate thing to do. Of the seven days, he worked four of them at the store and I worked the other three. He decided we should switch off and take turns so that whoever was not at the bookstore was at home keeping an eye on Denise.

Benson and his wife had been kind enough to let me stay with them after Nicholas's death seeing as I had nowhere else to go. I ended up permanently sticking around since Denise fell ill again with the same problems, she had faced years ago – which trailed all the way back to the time when I first met Benson.

I enjoyed spending time with her and she loved having me around – another lady to overpower decisions with Benson and a soft heart to help keep her positive during the healing process. This time though, there was not much the doctors could do for her. Apparently, she had gotten lucky before but I hardly believed that. How could you call someone lucky when their illness returns once more?

The only advice they could give her this time was to begin a natural body cleanse which consisted of nothing but garden-grown food and above all – lots of greens to fill her plate. On her good days, we would sit outside and read, enjoying my terrible tea and her sensational cookies. The bad days however were as one would expect – dark and gloomy. We spent most of those hours in the bedroom hovered over a bowl and keeping the cloth rag cold.

They had three children but none of them were willing to come and help their mother. Denise told me they hadn't visited in ages and she had given up hope long ago that they would come home. I learned that their absence wasn't entirely her fault – it was Benson's, *shocker*. He had an addiction problem – which she kept it at that – and when times were tough and he treated her badly – she stayed. The children remembered seeing this as they grew up and endlessly begged her to leave when they were old enough to know better but she wouldn't, she couldn't. She loved him; Benson was the love of her life. They had been through thick and thin together and marriage was for better or for worse and she meant that when she married him. Because of this, they stayed away from both their mother and father.

I could relate to Denise. She and I were similar in the way that we both had been treated badly and came out on the other side. We both had negative experiences but wouldn't or couldn't leave. The love that we had for our significant other kept our feet planted firmly there. I could only hope that Benson treated her better than Nicholas had treated me throughout the years.

Obviously, I didn't know what Benson was like back then but now, today he was a changed man and changing more every day. Of course, he had his corks and edges but we all do. If only their children could see him for the man he had grown into now. What the years had molded him into. Everyone deserved a second chance...right?

The thought was funny coming from me because I wouldn't have given Nicholas a second chance if I would've known from the beginning that it was him. I guess some things die hard. I could hear the familiar *ding* coming from the bell hanging on the door. It consistently rang behind me.

"Hey– uh. I just wanted to thank you for coming in to work today to help out. That is very much appreciated. I was really starting to fall behind keeping the shelves restocked with all the customers we've had lately. Old timers can only keep up with so much around here." *Some things never change.* Benson still couldn't look me in the eye when he was paying me a compliment. That was okay because he made me laugh inside – but it didn't mean I was going to go easy on him either.

"Oh, so you appreciate me huh? That's pretty much what I heard you say." I shot the biggest grin in his direction knowing well that he would be wearing a frown on his.

"No. That's not what I said. Don't you listen to a *dang* word I say? The *action* was appreciated. That's all." He briskly turned from me and walked back to the counter but his back didn't face me quick enough to not catch the small smirk that had grown on his face.

"Hey, Benson I finished putting all the books back that had been pulled out of their places. If that is all you needed me for, I'm going to head home and check on Denise."

"That'll be alright. I'll see you later on tonight," he said gently as he scratched the side of his face.

Their home wasn't too far from the bookstore. I'd say a good two miles away. For this, I was thankful at night when I was by myself locking up. To pass the time I would usually borrow a book from the store that I had my eye on and begin reading it while I walked home. But that was me, always having my nose in a book.

I loved their little house. It was a cottage setting that sat back in one of the only rural areas on the outskirts of the city. Denise had lined both sides of the walkway to the front door with flowers – hydrangeas to be precise. Two perfectly straight lines from the mailbox to the porch welcomed you with purple happiness. The backyard held a small creek – a steady flow of water rushing down through the land.

In the spring Denise and I would sit outside late at night with our hot chocolate and our blankets and listen to the peeper frogs as they spoke to one another in the darkness. Their discussions mixed with the sound of the water was the most calming thing I had ever heard.

The smell of the hydrangeas stuck with me well into the foyer as I headed in to check on everything. "Denise! I'm home!" I waited a minute or two – while I hung up my coat – to listen to the sound of her greeting me back. But that sound never came. This time I called out her name a little louder in case she was sitting out on the back porch – which on the good days is where I would find her. "Denise?"

A second time with no response had me panicking. I frantically ran through the usual rooms that I knew her to be in. One of which was her painting room. Through my continued search, I found no trace of her. Heading for the stairs, I sprinted to the top.

"Den–" Upon entering the bedroom, I found the normally spotless room to be in a bit of disarray. The bed sheets were a jumbled mess and the table on her side of the bed had fallen to the floor along with everything we had laying on it. As I rounded the bed to pick it up that's when I saw Denise laying there on her side with her face hanging down to the floor. Her bowl had been dumped out – leaving her laying in chunks of vomit. "DENISE!"

Her nightgown was soaked as if she had soiled herself and she had a large gash on her forehead – blood was steadily streaming from it. Seeing all this led me to believe that when she fell, she must've knocked herself unconscious.

The first thing I did was check her for a pulse which she did have. It was faint but that was more than enough heartbeat for me. I wasn't sure if I should move her for fear of hurting her worse so I decided not to.

Whispering in her ear I said, "Denise…I hate to leave you but I have to go get help. If you can hear me, I'll be back. I'll be back with help and we are going to get you to a hospital. Everything's going to be okay." I slid the hair hanging down in front of her face so I could see her eyes.

Fast Forward:

It had been two weeks since Denise's accident. She had been in a coma ever since we found her so no one knew for certain what exactly happened. She would be the only one to tell us the events of that day – whenever and if ever she woke up. From the pieces of information, I gave to her doctor he believed that she tried to get up to use the bathroom when she possibly felt dizzy while trying to use the table to stabilize her but instead, she toppled over it, losing her balance and hitting her head.

Benson had me picking up more shifts at the bookstore since they admitted Denise into the hospital – where she would remain until she woke from her sleep stage. There no longer was a reason for me to be home and he wanted to spend as much time sitting with her and reading to her as he could. I thought that was a good idea that one of us stay with her since she could one day open her eyes. And it was sad to think she could possibly do that on a day that no one would be there. Neither of us wanted her waking up and being alone. I could even bear the thought of it.

I found the distance to be good for Benson and me as well. When he was at the bookstore he wasn't really there. His body physically stood there but no one was pulling the strings. Understandably his mind was somewhere else.

He was aggressive when he was there. Not towards the customers as much – when he got irritated with them, he simply walked away and asked me to finish taking care of them. Which was a good thing to do because he didn't want to ruin the image of himself, he had worked so hard to build. And he didn't want to hurt the reputation of the bookstore either – it had come so far, accomplished so much and it would've been a shame to see it go downhill again. If it ever did, I feared that would be the last time this bookstore would ever see customers' faces.

Mainly the problem was that he was aggressive with me. Yelling about every subject he could. Sometimes he was venting to me but a lot of the time he was treating me rather badly – talking down to me and whispering profanities. I didn't blame him still – sadly I understood. I tried my best to shake it off when we did have exchanges like that.

Chapter V

Trailed

The last time I saw Benson he had screamed at me for allowing a few of the sconces to burn out on the upper floor. And although I apologized until I burned out the words, *I'm sorry* it didn't matter. To him, in his mind – I should have been doing my rounds and keeping an eye on everything as he does.

I didn't have the heart to tell him but truth be told those sconces were burned out well before I started running the bookstore without him. They were out the first day I arrived back. And I know for a fact that I mentioned it to him because of his *new bookstore image* but he obviously must have forgotten due to the volume of business and everything going on at home with Denise. Sadly, I understood that too. So instead of arguing back I just decided to let him get away with this one too.

Finding that we had no more in stock he gave me the name of a shop not far from the bookstore so that I could walk to it during my lunch break. He told me to tell the owner that he sent me and that the owner would give me a discount because he owed Benson for the *Clementines*. Whatever those were.

He told me to use that word if I should run into trouble. Normally we would never close the bookstore for lunch. We would simply stop eating to help the customers if need be but since this situation we were in was more delicate than usual he allowed me to hang a sign on the door and run the errand he needed me to.

I jiggled the handle for the third time while reading the *out to tea be back soon* sign that I had hanging on the door before departing. Turning quickly to start on my way I ran harshly into a man whose body seemed to be made of stone.

"I am *so* sorry! Please forgive me!" the man could barely speak the words as he knelt down to gather all the drawings he had dropped during our run-in. He grew increasingly irritated with his satchel that kept sliding down in front of him as often as he would slide it behind his back. Every move his body made as did his satchel. "I do beg your pardon! But you are the librarian here?"

"The what? No. I'm not a librarian. I am simply running the store during my boss's absence." I looked the man up and down not liking him already. I could smell the arrogance pouring from his skin – he reeked of it.

"Well then, in that case – I would like to see the books you have on building please." The man stood

43

with his chest puffed out and his shoulders back in an authoritative manner but that did nothing to sway me one way or the other.

"Building?" I asked a little confused. "I will need more detail than that sir."

"Ah– yes, well I am an engineer you see and I am working a job with a head contractor and his crew. I am trying to wrap my head around a project that I think should be done one way while he assures me it should be done another. And having not a lot of field experience in this yet I would like to look to the books if you will. Book smart you know." He tapped on his temple in a way that made me want to roll my eyes at not only the way he held himself but his attitude as well.

"Excuse me sir for it is I who is in need of sharing with you an apology. I have somewhere I have to be and it most certainly cannot wait. I shall return in one hour and by then the bookstore will be reopened for you to find the literature you are searching for. Good day." And without giving him the slightest chance to protest I marched in the opposite direction towards my destination.

As I walked, I noticed a car parked not that far away from the bookstore. It was one I had never seen before. Its color was a tad different from the others making it a little easier to stand out against the rest.

Inside I could make out two shadows occupying both front seats but no other detail to them than that. I got an antsy feeling – a tingling feeling that something wasn't right about this mystery car. There was something almost wrong about it. It made my skin crawl. I used the daylight to my advantage and picked up the pace until I was close enough to a crowd of people in case I needed help.

Before I knew it *The Bearded Bulb* electrical repair store stood before me looking almost as run-down on the outside as *The Page Turner* used to. The inside however was immaculately clean and organized. There was not a fixture out of place, a bulb bin empty, or a wire not perfectly banded.

"Can I *help* you?" a man abruptly asked, loud enough for the back of the store to hear. He was a tall man who wore a thick black mustache professionally on his upper lip.

He used the counter as if his arms were a kickstand and the top was the ground as he leisurely leaned. The air was filled with the smell of tobacco, so much so there was almost a haze around us – the smoke circling like a cloud. He had burned down one cigar in an ashtray next to his hand. While the one between his fingers he smashed the remaining tip before lighting the new one he already held between his lips.

"Uh– hi…are you the owner?"

"Who's asking?" he replied, appearing a little annoyed at the question.

"Well…you see…my boss sent me to get replacement bulbs for our store's sconces and he told me to ask for the owner."

"Yeah, yeah, ok. Sure, I'm the owner. The name is Edoardo. Now what kind of bulbs?" he looked at me with a serious *no bullshit* face.

Shit. "I…don't have the slightest clue actually. I'm sorry."

"Well, that presents a problem, doesn't it?" he asked almost rhetorically, puffing hard on his newly lit cigar.

"Um…I don't know if this is going to help you or not but my boss is Benson from the bookstore down the way and he sent me up here to get them. He said he knows you."

"Did he now? Well, how does he know me?"

Shit.

"I…uh–"

"Relax! I'm just messing with you! Yeah, sure I know Benson. That old son of a bitch. And you work for him huh? God bless you. He's an old jack getting off the roof if you know what I mean." He erupted into a wild laugh. "I'll grab those bulbs for you. Benson usually orders a few boxes so I always keep it stocked for him and whenever he's ready he usually just stops down and gets them. Speaking of the old fart. Where the hell is he? And *how* the hell is he?"

"Denise is very sick. He is having me look after the shop in his absence."

"That's terrible to hear," he said pulling the cigar from his mouth to shake his head towards the ground. "Please tell him I said if he needs anything he knows where to find me."

Setting the boxes down on the counter he read me the price off by memory. "Oh...and Benson said you would give me a discount..." I attempted to mutter under my breath without looking him in the eye.

"That son of a bitch. I can't believe he sent you in here to say that to me. He's a sneaky little prune I'll tell you. Anything to squeeze every last penny out of someone."

He took a minute to stop and look down at the bulbs while giving a few more puffs of smoke from the cigar before answering. I was filled with nervousness that he would yell at me with his booming voice like Benson had been doing lately. Inside I cursed myself for saying anything at all. I should've just paid the full amount and taken whatever extra it was out of my money to pay Benson back.

But I figured since that part already came out of my mouth I might as well finish with the rest of it. "He said you owe him for the *Clementines.*"

"Owe him for the box of Clementine's? That son of a bitch! He said those cigars were a gift. This is exactly why I don't accept them from anyone but myself." He pounded his fist down on the countertop, frustrated and admitting defeat.

Afterward, he gave me the bulbs at a discounted price and I thanked him for that repeatedly. "You don't have a beard," I randomly blurted out in the hopes of changing the conversation and lightening his mood while he gathered my change and packaged the bulbs in a bigger box for me to carry.

"A what?" he asked sternly. "Now don't tell me this is another one of Benson's comments because I have had about enough of him today."

"The shop…it's called *The Bearded Bulb*…but you don't have a beard and you are the owner…so what's with the name?"

"For your information little lady, I am the owner now but I'm not the original owner. It used to be called *Bob's Bulbs.* Bob had a beard and I wanted to try to keep the name close to its roots if you know what I mean."

"Oh…" I said pulling down the box from the counter. "What happened to Bob?"

"His bulb burnt out. He wasn't really an electrician. He had done some time and messed around with some electrical things while he was locked up. He thought that meant he could run his own electrical store. Boy did he find out more than a thing or two!"

I simply lifted my head in a surprising yet confusing way and headed for the door – thanking him once more and saying goodbye.

"Oh, and one more thing. You tell that son of a bitch he owes me now!" he shouted after me as I stepped out the door.

Making my way down the sidewalk I noticed that the same car from outside the bookstore was now parked on the opposite side of *The Bearded Bulb*. Was I being followed? I decided to take a detour into the gun shop a few doors down from Edoardo's place. Hoping that with any luck they would see me going in here, thinking I was going to purchase a gun and drive off. It was worth a try – after all, it couldn't hurt.

"Good afternoon! Welcome to *Automatic Relief!*" a stalky man greeted me warmly. "Can I help you find something today?"

I could easily see that this man took his job very seriously. If his full suit and tie wouldn't have been a clue then the fact that he was already pulling out a few examples to put on the counter for display would have given it away.

"No thank you. I am just browsing for the moment," I said kindly.

"May I ask what you will be browsing for today? Are we talking pistols and revolvers or shotguns and rifles?"

"It would be in the pistol family. But I am not looking to buy today – I am simply looking."

"No problem! My name is Leonardo and I'll be around if you need any help!"

After he finished putting his samples away, I saw the one that I knew would be my next gun. It was a blacked-out Colt 1911. And that beautiful specimen of a firearm had my name written all over it.

"Excuse me Leonardo…may I hold this one here please?" I asked as I pointed to the powerful pistol of my dreams.

"Nice choice, very nice indeed. This beauty is a forty-five-caliber single-action semi-automatic pistol. And here is the magazine," he said popping it from the base of the gun.

"Can you hold it for me until tomorrow?" I asked, knowing that Benson would be at the bookstore covering for a few hours in the morning. That should leave me with plenty of time to slip off, get the gun, and hide it safely away at home.

"Sure can," he said with a genuine smile. Waving goodbye, I think the two of us were both satisfied with the outcome.

When I reached the outdoors once more, the car was gone. I was thankful for that since everyone had seemed to disperse themselves finding that lunch was quickly coming to a close. I picked up the pace to get back to the bookstore. That's all I needed was for Benson to randomly stop by and catch the store being closed longer than he had permitted.

"Hey Abriana!" a voice shouted from my right as I made my way down the sidewalk. It was an older man who kept a protective eye on me. He was more of a caring uncle than a protective father. But he was a nice man, always working hard doing something – no one ever spoke a bad word about him. Rumor around was he used to be a teacher before he eventually retired and moved here to start a new chapter in his life. To me, that last part sounded familiar.

Chapter VI

Shadows

"Hey Lloyd!" I said warmly, trying my best to shout so he could hear me over the ruckus of what he and a few other men were moving. They were pushing a grand piano across the street to get to the sidewalk where I was standing and even among the horns and screams, nothing seemed to faze them. "Where have you been stranger? And where in the world are you going with that large piece?"

"Second floor – the apartment above the bookstore," he said with excitement. It made me smile to see his eyes light up. He was easily in his fifties and still seemed to be enjoying every bit of life in these streets. "I wanted to tell you I finished my painting collection we spoke of a few weeks ago. A buyer is coming to look at them this afternoon. That's what has kept me indoors for so long. I just had to finish it and so that's exactly what I did!"

"That's fantastic!" I said, giving him a quick hug. I could see over his shoulder that the two other men he was with had started wrapping rope around the piano to hoist it up to the second-floor window that had a larger balcony on the outside.

"I'd better help them out!" He pointed to the guys behind him who were almost finished with the rigging. "But it was great to see you, as always Abriana!"

"Don't stay away so long Lloyd. I'll be seeing you again soon," I said, wishing him well as I strolled past him to unlock the door of the bookstore.

The engineer was promptly back waiting by the side window, either that or he had been standing here the whole time and never left since our first encounter. I would say he was persistent but I think that was just the way of an engineer-type profession. "Hello again," he said with an extended hand.

"Hello to you too and I'm sorry my hands are full," I said looking down at the one unlocking the door and the other holding the box of bulbs.

Upon entering the man tripped on nothing but the air beneath his shoes and tumbled to the ground in front of me. Yet again scattering his drawings across the floor. But although his actions would seem like that of a clumsy fool it did not stop his arrogance from reemerging.

I hadn't even pulled the key from the hole before he started rushing me about where the building books are – to which I replied top floor

54

section D. I watched as the man walked to the door at least a dozen times – spitting outside of it – claiming that the smell of tobacco coming from my clothing was overwhelmingly powerful. And he couldn't stand inhaling it.

Suddenly the door abruptly slammed behind me, making me spin quickly to see what was happening.

"Where the *HELL* have you been?" an extremely large man in height and build screamed at the engineer. "I have been waiting on those drawings for OVER an hour?"

"I do apologize Ossa. I am merely trying to ensure that the vision you have aligns with the specific drawing details that I have."

"Every minute you WASTE time searching the pages of a book my men and I lose wrench time and that means losing the potential of finishing the project when it's SUPPOSED to be done. Now get your ASS back to the worksite immediately or I will break both of your legs so that you have to permanently stay there until the construction is completed! I have been doing this a lot longer than you have. Before you were even born! So, I think I should know the right and wrong way of going about things in this business. My father started this crew when I was eighteen years old and built it into what it is today. You're just a rookie."

When he turned his back on us, I could see that the print on his shirt read *C&C Construction established in 1905 – 45 years of experience guaranteed.* Ossa slammed the door once more – this time on his way out, striking up a match just outside the door to light his cigarette.

The engineer fumbled with his pile of books as he bounded down the staircase and over to the counter. "Just these," he said with haste.

I watched as he rushed out the door to get back to work. Something in my head told me to follow so I did. Stepping outside I saw Lloyd standing back at a distance staring up at the balcony. I met his side to follow his eye line.

"OSSA!" I heard the engineer shout after the man across the street. Pulling my attention away from the balcony. He fumbled with his books once more as he fought them to get across the street. Out of nowhere, a car came – hitting the man and sending him flying towards the side of the sidewalk where I stood before speeding off in the direction it was heading. The pile of books the man once struggled to gain control of now flew through the air like birds. "Ossa…I can't feel my legs I think they are broken…"

The victim was confused as he spoke to us as if we were Ossa. But he was standing on the other side of the road, waiting cautiously to get across. The engineer used his arms to crawl the rest of the way on to the sidewalk before flipping himself on his back to stare up at us.

"LOOK OUT!" Lloyd shouted just as the ropes gave way, leaving the piano come crashing down on the man – smashing his upper half to nothing.

I screamed as Lloyd rushed to his side but it was too late. It all happened so fast. Ossa was at my side covering my eyes from the view – but it was too late – I already saw the worst of it. I could hear Ossa and Lloyd shouting about something though it sounded muffled to me.

"Did you know this man?" I heard Llyod ask Ossa.

"Yeah...I knew him. He worked with my construction crew. I tried to take him under my wing since he was my niece's husband but after he broke her heart, I lost all sense of patience with him. He was ridiculous, all he ever cared about was the money – not the quality, which is something that never quite sat well with me. The structure he wanted to build was completely wrong and yet all he wanted to do was argue about it."

"Well...don't say that to the cops when they come or they'll think you had something to do with

57

it," Lloyd explained. "That sounds like a motive to me."

They exchanged a common look as if to silently say to one another that they were both thinking the same thing. A noise came from the streets sounding like a large truck. Glancing over a man jumped out of a garbage truck and came jogging over to Ossa and Lloyd. "Hey guys! What's going on Ossa?" As he asked the question, the two men who had helped Lloyd were moving the piano off of the engineer. "Is that who I think it is?" He pointed to the satchel next to the body.

"Yes…yes, it is Giasone," Ossa said to the garbage man trailing off into thought.

"Do you want me to uh–" he motioned towards the bed of the garbage truck.

"Between us," he said to Lloyd – both stating it and questioning it.

Lloyd looked to his two men who had their fingers on their noses like the sign of a secret. "Between us," he repeated.

"Giasone – if you wouldn't mind uh–" Ossa said.

"Say no more – the less we speak the better," he said as he whistled to the other garbage men in the truck who came running to his side. Together they hoisted what was left of the body, throwing it into

58

the bed of the truck followed by all the broken pieces of the piano.

"I'd say we are even now," Giasone whispered to Ossa.

"For now…" he said in reply.

The two men helping Lloyd had disappeared and reappeared before I even knew what happened. They were dumping buckets of water on the sidewalk and using scrub brushes to wash any evidence of what was once there. In the blink of an eye, we had gone from a crime scene to a cleanup and back to normal again. But that was the life of the members of the mafia.

A horn sounded next to us once more just as the last bit of evidence had been disposed of. "Hey Ossa!" a man parked next to the sidewalk yelled over. He was driving a 1932 Ford 5-window coupe and hanging out the passenger side window was the cutest long-haired dachshund I had ever seen. She had a feminine color collar on signifying that she was a little girl.

Ossa walked to the window – being sure to give the excited puppy some love. "Hey Giacomo," he said with a low voice.

"That piece of junk I've been working on over at my garage is going to need more parts than what I initially thought once I started tearing that stuff apart. I'm going to need more money to do that then what you gave me. Just drop it off when you have it."

"Ok, thanks for letting me know. I'll stop over when I get it," Ossa said before Giacomo pulled away from the sidewalk waving goodbye as he did.

I couldn't tell anyone about what had happened so it was my job to return to the bookstore and carry on a normal day as if nothing had happened. The crime itself didn't shake me as that hadn't been the only murder I had been around. It was the crunching sound of the bones snapping that did it for me. It took me back to my accident with Travis. The year of rehabilitation. The windshield. The memory left my legs shaking once more.

Fast Forward:

I was glad when the day came to a close. Benson never did come back to the bookstore the rest of the day which had me wondering what was going on with Denise. A late customer had come in – a mother and her child in need of a new book for bedtime reading. I couldn't turn her away so I left them in even though I was supposed to be locking up for the night.

By the time she had left, the clock read well past nine and it was pitch dark out. I always had to put my keys in the lock before turning out the lights and shutting the door, otherwise, when I got outside, I couldn't see the keyhole.

The same car was parked outside the bookstore again just like it had been earlier that day. It was now that I wished I had the gun in my bag. I glanced over only once not wanting to make a lot of unnecessary eye contact and draw too much attention to myself. Again, two shadows were sitting in the front seat of the car.

Rushing around the corner I made it down the next street without hearing the sound of an engine behind me. When I got to a safer distance, I looked over my shoulder to see if the car was following me, which it did not appear to be. Collecting a breath of fresh air, I felt relieved as I entered the cottage and locked myself safely inside for the night.

It didn't look like Benson was home considering the house was dark and there wasn't the slightest sound coming from inside. I made my way around the rooms and turned on the usual lights before heading upstairs to take a bath and clean up for bed. I took a minute to go into their room to make absolutely sure he wasn't home. When I flicked the light switch on, I could see their bedroom was a disaster.

There were papers thrown all over the floor, all the drawers hung wide open, the bed sheets were flipped off the bed – even the mattress hung off of it slightly. Benson would have never left their room like this – not even if he was in a hurry. For fear of upsetting Denise when she came home from the hospital.

After closing all the drawers, I fixed the mattress and bedsheets. I had begun picking up the papers when the doorbell rang. I grabbed the baseball bat that I kept from my old apartment when I lived above the Greco's because whoever was here was certainly not Benson. And at this time of night, I wasn't quite sure what their intentions were.

When I looked out the front window, I saw no one standing on the porch by the door, nor did I see anyone walking down the path. I gripped the bat hard in the opposite hand as I slowly unlocked one bolt at a time with the other – pausing in between the two to listen against the door for any sound. Cautiously I opened the door. But as I had previously suspected no one was there.

Instead, was a paper folded in half laying on top of the door mat. Peering around at the surroundings I saw no other evidence of a person or vehicle nearby. Grabbing the paper, I quickly locked myself back inside the house.

Sweat began to soak my armpits as I nervously held the object. My hand shook uncontrollably and my breathing quickened. I flipped open the paper and found nothing inside of it. It contained no writing of any kind. I rushed to the window to look outside again but there was still nothing there. *Someone was clearly taunting me.*

I turned all the lights off downstairs and bounded for the staircase locking myself inside my room – changing my mind about getting a bath tonight. To me, it felt too vulnerable if someone was indeed out there. I climbed into bed and held the bat tight to my chest as I continued to listen for any noises outside the house.

Chapter VII

Traceable

The following morning, I was awoken by something that sounded like two engines running. Outside the bedroom window, I saw two cars racing down the driveway towards the house. One was a medical vehicle while the other was a mail carrier. Heading outside to meet them the two were chatting and laughing about something being shared just between the two of them, barely noticing I was there.

"I didn't even see you, Roberto!" the mail carrier said laughing.

"You can say that again Sharon! I've been chasing after you the whole way since main street!"

"You know me…as soon as I get in that car the radio goes up and the gas pedal goes down!" she laughed again until tears came to her eyes.

"Oh, hey Abriana!" Roberto said finally noticing me. "Here are the medications the doctor prescribed for Denise to take when she gets home. Since I had to do a run for another patient, I told Benson I would take care of delivering them to the house."

"Thank you so much, Roberto. I'll put this inside for them." During the conversation, I noticed

Sharon putting a single envelope in the mailbox as she turned to look at me and smiled.

Waving them goodbye I heard Sharon say, "Want to race back?"

Roberto laughed in his vehicle as he revved the engine. "Ready, set, GO!" he shouted.

I watched them race up the driveway – kicking up a pile of dust until they were out of sight. Once they were gone, I took a trip down to the mailbox – forgetting to grab what Sharon had put inside – before returning to the house to get ready for the day and head to *Automatic Relief* to pick up my pistol.

Fast Forward:

The car was again parked outside of the bookstore as I made my way past to get the pistol. This marked two days they were following me, stalking me. I arrived at the gun shop merely minutes after they opened. Leonardo packaged up the gun for me while I counted out all the money, laying it on the countertop.

When I left the gun shop the car had followed its usual disappearing act. Checking the watch that hugged tight to my wrist I picked up the pace in order to make it back home and to the bookstore before Benson chewed my head off for being late. I was due to arrive at work no later than ten o'clock. Benson had been there since eight – opening the store for those customers that woke with the sun. Believe it or not, there was a lot of business first thing in the morning. Many of our customers were rushing for their nine a.m. arrivals to their own jobs, merely stopping to grab a piece of literature to occupy them during their lunchbreaks.

I arrived home at precisely nine o'clock, giving me plenty of time to figure out where I was to hide the gun and then get back to the store. I went about my usual morning routine, acting as if I had just gotten up for the first time and was getting ready for the day ahead of me. It was the only way to keep myself organized enough in my head not to forget where I need to go, what I need to do, and any of my belongings before leaving.

Placing my purse on the kitchen table as I had done every morning – the envelope from earlier caught my attention. With the rush of trying to get to *Automatic Relief* just as soon as they opened – to handling Denise's medication – I hadn't noticed anything about it prior to this moment. It was addressed to me in a handwriting I did not recognize. A strange feeling came over me, the same as when the taunting blank paper had arrived on the porch in the middle of the night. A sudden urge to open it filled my veins. Checking the watch on my wrist for what seemed like the ten thousandth time, only five minutes had passed. Plenty of time to open the envelope, hide the gun, and get to work.

and may the smell of the burning
bring you back to the day
may the flames of the night
haunt you while you lay
may the remnants of the morning
make you remember the betray
may the loss
make you wish to stay

My hands began to shake, along with my body, and my mind. There was a pit in my stomach, I was getting physically sick. How could anyone know? No one was there...no one saw me? Unless they had discovered there was a body missing – my body. Only one was to be found in the rubble and it was not that of a lady.

What would become of me? They are coming for me. And by the looks of it, they are getting closer and closer each day. I had nowhere to run. I couldn't go to the police because then I would have to confess...or would I?

Could I pull off an extravagant enough story to dig myself out and stay alive still? Could I somehow pin it back on them? *This is crazy! They would never get blamed for this crime and I know that!*

I'm never going to get away with this. I was a fool thinking I could. Now the only thing left to do was to wait for whatever punishment would come my way from this. Every action equaled a consequence and it was time to pay mine.

The only choice I had was to keep the note on my person. I couldn't very well leave it here for Benson to find – or Denise in her fragile state! So, shoving the note deep in my purse I continued with what I came to do. As I ascended the stairs to my room all I could think about was the note. I could see the words sitting on every step as I climbed higher and higher.

Burning. Flames. Remnants. Betray.

The power in the words sent chills up my spine. By the time I reached my room, my preoccupied mind couldn't remember what I was there for. Before long I remembered holding something in my hand – a box. That held a powerful weapon perfectly concealed and awaiting my next decision.

The bedroom that I called my home was the eldest son's room. Benson had high hopes of him taking over the bookstore one day. Seeing as he was considered the second man in the house – should anything ever happen to their dear father of course. And because of this Benson had an in-floor safe cemented into the boards of his bedroom. Where he had kept his own gun at one time.

He never gave me the combination but I was able to use my stethoscope to break the code – a skill my brother had taught me years before his murder. Uncovering the safe from under the rug I quickly opened the door and put the box inside – leaving it unopened along with the small pack of bullets he had banded to the outside of the box.

After obsessively checking my watch, time had somehow escaped me somewhere between the stairs and the combination lock. These simple tasks had accounted for thirty minutes of the stolen time. I now had half an hour to get from home to work. With the bookstore being every bit of two miles away I would be cutting it very close and that was *if* I left right now. Bounding down the staircase I jogged to the kitchen to grab my purse before heading out the door in a hurry.

"How is Denise?" I asked Benson, trying my best not to sound breathless after the last bit of my trip to work had turned into a full-blown jog. "I was worried when you didn't stop back into the bookstore the other day and then you didn't come home."

"It was a bad night Abriana. One of many that have been occurring more frequently lately. The doctors have now officially declared there is nothing more they can do for her. They had made the statement before but they weren't completely sure how true that was. Well, now they have come to the conclusion..." He hung his head just as the tears began to fill his eyes. He sniffed hard and with it I could hear all the crunching of the snot being pushed back up into his nostrils.

I gave him some time to finish his sentence before I spoke, knowing well that he was in a delicate state. But I could see by his facial expression that he was lost. Either lost in thought of what to say next or just completely lost by the entire situation. After what seemed like a long time I decided to begin delicately – coasting him back to our conversation. "And…"

He took a deep breath before answering. Allowing the air to fill his lungs entirely before releasing it all at once. "And they think that during this time it will be better for her to be at home during these final days."

"F–final days?"

Benson broke out into tears as I struggled to choke the words out. "The hospital will be sending a live-in nurse to stay with us after I bring her home. To help make her time here as comfortable as possible. They want her to be surrounded by people who love her and in the home she adored. They think it will help ease her mind. And help keep everything as calm as it can be."

"But they sent home all kinds of medication! A bag of it in fact!" I began to cry while the news sunk in more and more.

He shook his head side to side at least a dozen times. "That's only to help with the pain, nausea, and a few other side effects that will come during this."

"Should you…send for the children?" I asked barely breathing at the thought of her dying without getting to see them one last time.

"I did…but I haven't yet received a response. I have no hope that they will come. I didn't even bother telling Denise that I had reached out. It would only get her hopes up only to hurt and disappoint her once more when they didn't show. I can't have any more unnecessary pain come to her than what already will."

I continued to sob as he gathered the few items he needed before heading off. "I need to stop by the house and get rid of these dirty clothes of hers and pick up a fresh pair for her to wear. I will be bringing her home tomorrow sometime in the morning."

Rubbing my hand up and down his arm I said, "I'll make sure the bed is down and ready for her."

"That would be appreciated. Thank you Abriana. We'll see you then."

I placed a small, quick kiss on his cold, wrinkly cheek although I think he hardly noticed. He was gone – somewhere else entirely. Maybe he had never truly left the hospital. Maybe there he still stood in her room hovering over her, kissing the top of her head or sitting in the chair next to her bed rubbing her hand softly.

"Benson! Wait!" I shouted after him, remembering about a book I wanted him to read to her today. "Take this and read it to Denise tonight, will you? It's called, *For the love of a cure.* It's a love story about a woman dying of an uncurable disease. At the last minute...everything works out. Maybe this will give her a little hope and help with keeping her positive and at peace. And one more thing...please tell her I love her."

"I will dear. We'll see you tomorrow," he said hanging his head once more as he wiped the tears from his eyes.

I didn't know what he meant by that. Did he mean he would read it to her or he would tell her I loved her? Both I felt were equally important. I hoped very much he would read her the story. Even if he didn't believe in it – it wasn't about him, it was about her and I knew from all the time we had spent together that it would make all the difference in her eyes.

Chapter VIII

Sensical

The hours dragged on as if I worked more than one day. I couldn't help but think of Benson. I had never seen him that way before. He truly loved Denise with all of his heart even if he didn't always show it. I hoped more than anything their children would come. I know that would mean the world to her. She needed to see them, they needed to see her. And although the timing wasn't the best – it was better to be late than to have never come at all. It was high time they made up with their father. He would need them now more than ever and I felt as if they would need him too to some degree.

Finally, closing time fell upon me and I couldn't be more grateful. Checking my watch, I knew that there was no way the hospital would let me in to visit and if they did, she would no doubt be sleeping. A voice inside my head told me I should've gone earlier in the week but I felt unsure about doing it. I didn't want to step on Benson's toes or invade their privacy in any way. I didn't know how bad she really was and maybe she didn't even want me to see her like that.

Surprisingly the car that had been present was nowhere to be found tonight. I was grateful for that. I had too much on my mind and I couldn't worry about anything else. But as much as I tried to put everything out of my mind, I still felt like I was forgetting something...something important.

"Abriana!" a familiar voice called out my name from behind. "I thought that was you. Is the bookstore closed for the evening?"

Confusion fell over me as I found Matteo to be the one approaching from behind.

"Oh...Good evening, Matteo, and why...yes, it is..." I couldn't help but be stunned to see him but Antonio was nowhere to be found.

"You look confused or curious about something Abriana. I bet you're wondering what I am doing here."

"Truth be told I cannot account for the pleasure of running into you again." *Especially since I had high hopes of never seeing you or your partner again.*

"Well to tell *you* the *truth* Antonio and I have been transferred to this area. What a coincidence to find you at the same place." He pulled out a familiar-looking toothpick and began to chew away at it.

Attempting to shrug his pre-interrogation off, I yanked the key from the door in an irritated manner. "I beg to differ Matteo. I wouldn't call that a coincidence at all."

"What would you call it than Miss Abriana?" he asked in more of a mocking tone.

"A stroke a luck. For our great city to have your company." Even though I practically gagged at the sentence – kissing his ass might get him off mine.

He laughed a dirty laugh. One that was sick in nature but one that didn't believe a word that slithered past my teeth. Pushing the toothpick to the opposite side of his mouth with his tongue – he tipped his hat to me slightly. "Until we meet again. Goodnight Abriana." Just like that, he snuck away into the night – disappearing almost as quickly as he had appeared.

At the end that had been my goal, to insult him with a smile enough to get him to walk first – which he did. Whether he knew it or not I made the rules and he wasn't going to bully me into changing them – not for him, Antonio, or anyone else. I had come too far to not get caught and I wouldn't allow two snooping police men coming out of the woodwork to reveal my past.

I walked home in the most depressed mood I had felt in a long time. I hadn't been this low since I lost Danny and our unborn child.

At least now I could release all of the emotions I had struggled to hold in today so that I could uphold my professional demeanor. I wish I could say that I couldn't remember the last time I cried this hard but that would've been a lie. I remember clearly. The moment my tears began to flow all of the memories came back – flooding me with more emotion than I knew resided still within my body. But Denise was family and I couldn't imagine her not being there one day. We had grown so close and I couldn't even grasp it all. It just seemed so unfair. She was such a kind woman and I just didn't understand.

Fast Forward:

Rays of sunshine blinded my face, waking me from what seemed like a light sleep. I didn't remember anything about last night – not walking home, getting into the house, not even getting into bed. Everything had been a complete blur. My bones ached; my body was tired like I hadn't slept at all the night before.

Benson had been kind enough to allow me to close the bookstore today since Denise was coming

78

home. He knew I hadn't seen her and I think he too thought it was important for me to get to spend as much time as I could with her before the end. After getting ready I went outside to pick Denise's favorite flowers to welcome her home. I put a vase on the kitchen table so she could see them when she came in and one on her bedside table to look at while she was lying down. I knew they would make her smile, hopefully brightening her mood if she wasn't in a good one.

It didn't take me long to realize I had forgotten the book on the counter last night that I wanted to bring home to read to her today. A mistake that may not have occurred if I hadn't been distracted further by my run-in with Matteo. Checking my watch, it seemed I would probably have enough time to get there and get back before they arrive. Grabbing my purse, I took off in a mad rush.

On the final stretch to the bookstore, I could hear lots of voices – shouts, and screams echoing from all directions. Fire engines flew down main street before I had even reached the top of the corner. The air smelled of something so familiar – something charred.

"And we meet again Miss Abriana!" Matteo clapped his hands together as if I was being subtly charged with something. "Much sooner than I had expected!"

Although my attention had been pulled towards him upon my turn of the corner, I was quickly drawn towards the mixing colors of red, orange, and yellow that I could see from the side of my eye. I felt a temperature of heat consistent with what I imagined it would be like to stand in front of the sun.

"NOO–" I screamed so loudly that everyone turned to look at me. Out of instinct, I went running towards my beloved bookstore although it remained engulfed in the dying flames that the fire engines were trying so desperately to put out.

Matteo grabbed me by the back of my arms, pulling me in his direction so that I collided with him. "You can't go any closer Abriana! It's too dangerous! We have to wait until after the fire has been put out and the structure has cooled down enough."

Tears ran down my face, racing from my eyes like raindrops from a cloud. I heard what he said but I didn't want to. It made perfect sense but it didn't. I watched as Antonio stood in the street talking to various groups of bystanders who had gathered to watch the disaster. He took notes as they spoke.

"When did this happen?" I asked, shaking Matteo's hands off of me.

"We are not sure yet. That's what we are trying to figure out. Antonio has been questioning groups of people all morning to try to put the pieces together. We need to find out what started the blaze."

I almost shrieked in shock at his response. "All morning?"

"Yes, it was burning in the early hours is what we have been told thus far," he said, staring at me intently.

"You didn't happen to leave a light on or a candle burning, did you? Anything that may have caused it?"

Throwing my arms in the air I couldn't help but yell at him. "You have got to be kidding me! What? You think I might have done this! Absolutely not! There was no candle or light left on! This bookstore means the world to me – it's my life, my livelihood! I treat it as if it were my own!"

"Keep your voice DOWN!" This time he equaled my frustration. "I never said you were a suspect! It's just regulation for me to ask these questions! Afterall you were the last one here and if I can recall correctly, you weren't *exactly* in the right state of mind! Accidents happen, okay! That's

81

all I'm saying!" I watched as he stormed off to Antonio, pulling him from his ongoing conversation to talk with him alone about something private.

Before long I could see Antonio gawking in my direction and I knew that couldn't be a good thing. They exchanged a look I had seen before but did not yet know what it meant. Matteo whispered something to him which left Antonio creeping over in my direction.

"Hello again Abriana," he said when he reached within an arm's length of me.

"Getting all caught up with your stories?" I asked in a cocky way as I glared at him.

"No need to be hostile. Remember we are just trying to do our job."

"You're always *just trying to do your job* without really doing *your* job!"

"Is that what you think?" he asked so calmly it was terrifying. His eyes were cold, dark. And although we were surrounded by people, I felt that wouldn't stop him from attempting to hurt me. He walked a few more steps towards me – almost completely closing the gap between us. He was so close I could smell last night's alcohol on his breath – it blew in my face like the wind, prickling my nostril hairs as he spoke. "Let me see your bag...please."

"Excuse me? I'm not going to give you my b–"

In one swift move, he had ripped the purse off my shoulder and was tearing through it.

"HEY!" I shouted as I tried to reach for it. But he only kept dodging my attempts by turning one way and then the other. He was such a large man in size that it was difficult to do anything that would remotely help me.

"I asked you one time and I said please!" he almost shouted in my direction.

The minute he yanked that piece of paper from my purse I lunged at him. I knew what it was since it was the only loose paper I stored in there. If he read that they would find a way to hold it against me. I cursed myself for not burning the paper after I had read it. I knew better.

One hard push to my chest had hurled my body back against the closest wall of another shop. I slammed against its brick wall with such force, I felt and heard a part of my spine crack on impact. When I looked up the damage was done. He had read the letter and with it the envelope that held my name.

Sometime during the struggle, Matteo had joined his side and was now approaching me on his own. "Why...did you search...my bag?" I asked him between pauses – still trying to catch my breath from the wind being knocked out of me. I demanded an answer from him. This was my *personal* belonging. *My* private letter.

"You didn't even realize how suspicious you were acting – that is how out of it you are."

"Well EXCUSE me for being DISTRACTED! I didn't know that was against the law around here!" I said holding back tears. All I could think about was my dear Benson and my sweet Denise who was coming home today. This would kill them. I didn't want them to see me cry, I refused to let them see. Turning from them I wiped down my face with both of my hands to try and compose myself.

"That's not what I mean," Matteo said from behind me.

"Then WHAT do you MEAN?" I said, my tone sounding exasperated.

"You were holding on to that purse for dear life. You were squeezing the straps in your hand so hard that you were white-knuckled."

"And that led you to believe that I had something in my purse? That was *evidence* enough that you needed to search it?"

"No, but it was worth a try. I guess you could say it was just a lucky hunch. Weren't *you* the one who told me last night that the city was *lucky* to have us? I think you might've been on to something." His laughter was filled with arrogance

– it made me want to hit him. It made me want to punch him in the face as hard as I could, even if it meant breaking my hand to do it. "Now you can come down to the station like a nice girl without making a scene or we can do this the hard way. Isn't that right Antonio?"

Looking past Matteo, I could see Antonio swinging handcuffs in front of his chest. Quietly warning me of what would come next if I didn't go along with them willingly to the station.

"Where is the car?" I asked looking back to Matteo.

"That's a good girl," he said resting his hand gently on my back to guide me there.

Chapter IX

Circles

Twisting the paper cup on the table I waited impatiently for more questions. There was no clock or window in the room they held me in. So, I didn't know what time it was to even guess if Benson and Denise were home yet. The only piece of furniture occupying the room was a wide four-legged table with three chairs – one on one side and two on the other.

Alas, I could not take the silence a minute more. "Oh my– how many times do we have to go through this?" I yelled.

"As many times as it takes or until we tell you to stop."

Rolling my eyes I said, "I can only tell you what I know and not a detail more than that."

"Just a recap then, humor me Miss Abriana," Matteo pushed on unconvinced.

"It could have been addressed to anyone. There is no name on the letter. Do you hear what I am saying? My name isn't even on it! And I have already recapped a dozen tim–"

"That may be the case but the envelope itself was addressed to you and that my dear is *no* mistake. Your name was on the initial envelope was it not?"

I felt no need to answer since he was plainly holding the envelope almost directly in front of my face to ensure I had gotten a good look at it.

"So, you receive an envelope in the mail. This envelope to be exact – which contains no clue of who it was from on the outside. And the only detail that is written on it is your name and address. Is this statement correct thus far so that I may continue?" Matteo said matter-of-factly.

"It is!" I said in a snippy way, refusing to look up at him from the cup.

"And you say you have been being followed the past several days as well?" He looked to Antonio whose eyes were glued to the letter once more.

"I wasn't really followed per se, I was…I don't know what I was! All I know is the same unfamiliar car was parked outside where I work for many days. Then yesterday was the first day it just wasn't there."

"And you never saw the driver? Or anyone in the car for that matter?"

"Correct I never saw either of the two bodies that looked to be in the car." My eyes kept bouncing from his to Antonio who was still staring down at the letter.

Before Matteo could ask his next question Antonio slammed his fist on the table, throwing the letter down with it. "What does this *mean* to you?" his voice bellowed inside the four walls. "What do these *words* mean? Whoever is speaking to you obviously knows you so what are they talking about?"

I was so stunned that Antonio was smarter than he looked that I could only watch the paper spin on the table in circles. Hoping that he would simmer down. My first impression proved to be wrong about him he wasn't just the muscle behind the two of them, he also had some brains.

During my silence, Matteo stepped in – tapping his finger on the letter. "Well, he does have a point…" I flashed my eyes to his and to Antonio's to gauge their reaction.

"Tell us what you *know* – tell us what you're *hiding* or we will be forced to lock you up for withholding information during an investigation."

"As I told you before I can only tell you what I know and not a detail more than that."

"I think we have our answer," Matteo said looking at Antonio.

It was cold in the holding cell. I could feel the chill coming from the block walls and the concrete floor. It all reeked of mustiness and the strong stench of urine.

The small room was filled with bodies. However, I was the only one properly dressed or proper looking at all. Moving from the bench I began to pace the floor – trying to think up a story for when they came and got me to offer one more chance to tell them what I knew. *Think. Think. Think.* Searching the faces of the men who were stuck in here with me I found dirty fingernails, rotten teeth, death hands, and ripped clothes. I didn't belong here.

What would Denise and Benson think? Did they wonder where I was? Did anyone from the street see me leaving with the cops after the scene of the crime and tell them I was a suspect? Did they even know I was alive? Maybe they thought I died in the fire – perished with the building I so deeply loved. Even that would be almost better than this right now.

Instead, I found myself being held in a doghouse with people I shouldn't be around – I didn't belong in here and that was quite obvious. But I was in a situation I couldn't dig my way out of. My only way of escaping was to curl up against the cold concrete wall and slip away into my dreams.

Fast Forward:

In what seemed like a matter of a few minutes I heard the sound of keys clanging followed by a lock being unlocked. "Today must be your lucky day Abriana." Matteo stood facing me with the cell door wide open along with two fellow cops by his side that I had never seen before. Antonio was nowhere to be found. "Our captain has forced us to release you on the grounds of possessing unsubstantial evidence to charge you with. You are free to go…for now." Handing me my bag, he stepped out of my pathway leaving the two men standing by to escort me out of the building.

I barely knew how to walk on my own. My legs didn't work as they used to and neither did my mind. I didn't know what day it was or what hour. I hadn't seen the sun in days – felt its warmth on my face in ages. They had held me there for seven days. Seven days of three cups of water a day and two plates of dogfood along with only one bathroom break and zero phone calls or visitors. But who would call me or visit me? Nobody knew I was here – of that, I was sure. I could rot here and no one would know.

Matteo had said that with the weekend falling upon us when I was first being held that it pushed my release date back so that they could process everything. Personally, I didn't believe a word of that. I think that was just an excuse to keep me longer and see if I would crack under the pressure.

I arrived at the house late afternoon before the sun had turned to its evening setting. The stairs leading up to the porch and the porch itself were covered with bouquets of flowers and I didn't understand why. The house was quiet – too quiet like nobody was home.

After looking in every room on the main floor, I found no one to be there. The flowers were still on the kitchen table as I had left them a week earlier before everything happened. They too wilted with sadness and began to lose their petals and color. Deciding that maybe they are resting upstairs after a long day I made my way up the stairs. I called out Benson's name in almost a whisper but heard nothing back in response. Nothing out of the ordinary looked to have happened and nothing seemed to be out of place.

The sheets on their bed were still down and waiting for bodies to occupy them. They must be releasing her much later than what Benson had originally thought. Walking into my room I was about to gather clothes for a bath when I noticed something that I shouldn't have thought was strange

– considering I was the last person in that exact spot. The corner of my rug was crinkled up and I may not have noticed it if it weren't for the tassels being flipped back instead of laying down on the floor flat.

Pulling the rug back there was nothing odd to see regarding the safe itself but I opened it anyway. My pistol was gone as were all the bullets that were inside. I sat there in a state of shock. Staring into the safe as hard as I could – in disbelief that it was missing. In its place sat what looked to be a blood-soaked rag.

The doorbell suddenly rang unexpectedly pulling me from my thoughtless mind. Jumping up I ran for the door, forgetting to close the safe.

"Today is not your lucky day," Matteo said when I opened the door. One of the two cops who had escorted me out merely an hour ago was spinning me around and handcuffing me while I was being read my rights. The other cop disappeared farther inside the house.

"HEY! What are you doing? Let me go! What is all THIS about?" I yelled over my shoulder to Matteo.

"Miss Abriana you are under arrest for the murder of your employer, guardian, and landlord – a Mr. Benson–" Matteo said.

"WHAT? This is outrageous! He's at the hospital!"

"You have the right to remain silent. Anything you say can and will be used against you in a court of law. You have the right to an attorney. If you cannot afford an attorney, one will be provided for you. Do you understand?"

"Understand this!" I said as I spit in his face once the cop handcuffing me spun me around to face him.

"Very nice Abriana. Very nice indeed. I forgot how much of a lady you are," he said in response, pulling a handkerchief from his breast pocket to wipe his face off with.

"Hey! I got something up here!" the first cop yelled from the top floor.

"Bag it and bring it down!" Matteo yelled up to him. "Put her in the car."

"You won't get away with this!" I screamed over my shoulder to Matteo as the cop struggled to push me out the door. I fought as hard as I could against his strength – digging my feet into the floor to stop me from moving but nothing worked. He just kept kicking my legs and shoving me forward.

Fast Forward:

"Fingerprint her and book her – you know the usual process. Once she's done bring her into the interrogation room for questioning," I heard Matteo whisper to the cop who was still manhandling me.

"Does this room look familiar?" Antonio asked as he shined the light of the lamp directly into my eyes.

Turning my face from it I said, "Asshole!"

Hovering over the table he leaned in close. "I'm sorry what was that? I don't think I heard you correctly?"

"I said ASSHOLE!"

With a strike to the face, he slapped me hard. He moved so quickly that I didn't even have a chance to see his hand coming. Not that I could have done anything other than flinch. They had my hands cuffed behind my back to the chair. "No more miss nice girl huh? Now that you got caught."

"That's enough Antonio," Matteo said as he stormed into the room throwing a folder on top of the table.

"What?" Antonio asked confused by the interaction.

"SIT DOWN!" Matteo said.

I had to turn my face so they didn't notice me laughing at the two of them bickering back and forth. It would seem Matteo was coming back with the pants on now.

"What did you mean by he's at the hospital?" he said, flipping open the folder that contained several documents on one side and photographs on the other. I tried to stare hard at the pictures to see if I could make out what they were but since they were upside down it made it more difficult. Matteo snapped his fingers at me to regain my attention when I didn't answer his question.

"He's at the hospital with Denise..." I said with clenched teeth.

"Well, you're right about that?"

"And what is THAT supposed to mean?" I said in an outrage.

"You should KNOW!" Antonio said jumping down my throat.

"ENOUGH!" Matteo said, breaking the two of us up again.

I jolted forward pulling at the handcuffs against the chair. "He's supposed to bring Denise home today – she doesn't have very long to live and he's bringing her home."

Matteo stared down at the paperwork, scanning his eyes over all the words as if he wasn't listening to me. "No. Denise was supposed to be released seven days ago, remember? And where were you during the hour you were released from here?"

"I was at home – where you found me."

"Do you have an alibi to confirm your whereabouts at the time that the crime was committed?" He said, scanning his eyes over my face. Antonio stared at me too – not giving anything away about what he might be thinking.

"Uh – let's see Matteo, did you find anyone else in the house with me, or was I all by myself?" I said with a snarl. He chose not to answer my rhetorical question. "This is crazy. You have to know that. I was being held here."

"Not within the hour you weren't here and that was when it happened," Antonio said.

Matteo gave him a cross-eyed look as if to warn him one last time for taking over. Abruptly Antonio got up and slammed the door behind him – leaving the two of us alone.

"Here's the deal Abriana," he said slamming the folder shut. "Benson is dead. Shot, killed, *murdered* in cold blood. Now you claim you haven't seen him. But then you turn around and say things like he's at the hospital."

"HE IS!" I said screaming at him for not listening to me.

"YES, YOU'RE RIGHT HE IS! HE IS IN THE MORGUE AT THE HOSPITAL!" Pausing he took a few deep breaths before continuing. "Denise died yesterday in the afternoon. Benson was in the morgue privately viewing her body when someone came in, snuck up behind him, and shot him in the head."

"I don't believe you!" I said between tears.

Matteo spun the folder around to face me and flipped it open to reveal the contents inside. He turned the pictures over one by one and laid them out in a straight line in front of me to see.

I couldn't stand to look at them anymore so I twisted my face away. "Benson…" I said almost in a whimper as I cried into my shoulder. "I loved him like family! He was my family! And if you or anyone else in this wretched place thinks I killed him you can go to hell." Staring him down I let the tears continue to run down my cheeks – relentlessly continuing to glare at him.

"I'm sorry for your loss Abriana but this is not looking in your favor at all. The gun found at the scene of the crime was registered to you."

I stared at him blankly. Dumbfounded by what I just heard.

"Don't look so shocked we interviewed everyone within a mile of the bookstore during the fire including Leonardo. He happened to tell us that you were the last customer he had when he pulled his records to show us. This can't just be a coincidence. First the bookstore, then Benson and you are the only piece that fits both."

"I told you I was being followed! Someone is setting me up! Matteo please!" I said beginning to cry again.

"I'll ask you one more time – why did you kill Benson? If you plead guilty now, I will try to get you a lesser sentence. All you have to do is tell me why you did it."

"Burn in hell," I said wiping my cheek on my shoulder.

"I'm sorry you feel that way." Matteo got up and knocked on the door three times. "If the prints on the gun or the rag are a match to yours – you'll be going to prison for a long time."

When the door opened Matteo shook his head at the cop holding the door open. It was the same one who had handcuffed me earlier. This time he uncuffed me from the chair and escorted me to my jail cell.

Chapter X

Innocence

Almost two months had passed before any news came from the case at all. The last bit of information I was told was that the evidence would have to be sent to the crime lab in California – which was the other side of the country from where I was. Technology was not very well advanced so I had been told it would take two weeks for the evidence to even arrive and then at least another two to examine and another two to send back and that was if they gathered all the information that they needed within that time frame. Since this was the most trusted crime lab, they were swamped with evidence all being looked into and who knows what number mine was.

The door to my jail cell swung open early one morning. The only words I heard were, "Matteo wants to see you." The cop sat me in an empty interrogation room – this time with my hands cuffed to the table I was sitting at. I sat there quietly for a long time. Listening to nothing but the sound of doors slamming in the hallway.

Within the hour the door to the room opened revealing Matteo coming inside. "Okay I'm going to make this quick," he said without sitting down. "The prints on the rag weren't yours and only a partial print was found on the gun but it doesn't look to have matched yours. However, we were still keeping you even up until this point due to some other things being worked out but that was until thirty minutes ago when the judge set your bail due to this newly acquired documentation regarding the case. Within fifteen minutes of your bail being set – it was posted."

"P–posted?" I asked confused. "I'm afraid I don't understand.

He stepped forward and began unlocking the cuffs around my wrists. "You are free to go...once more," he said as he returned the key to his pocket. "Someone paid your bail so that you could leave – that is what it means. Now it has been highly recommended that we place you in the witness protection program but of course, the choice is yours. Just be aware that someone out there is obviously trying to frame you or kill you and they almost succeeded with one."

Swallowing hard I was escorted out of the jail once more – this time getting a ride back home by two cops who were almost off duty for the day. Waving them goodbye I first went to the mailbox which was overflowing with letters – mostly bills –

but one of which was addressed to me from Tucson, Arizona. Entering the house, it felt different. There was more than one thing missing and the air was so quiet that I could've heard a mouse squeak.

Dear Abriana,

My name is Jacqueline, you may know me as Benson and Denise's daughter. My brothers and I had planned to come down relatively soon to see our mother once we had received our father's message. But not only did the news reach us that it was too late to see her one last time, but we also came home to find that our father had been murdered.

At the funeral, we had been told by many flapping mouths that you were the one that was being charged for the crime. I could hardly believe it though. Our Mother had written us many letters saying nothing but good things about you.

Although my brothers were on the fence about me writing you this letter, I felt that it was the right thing to do. Thank you for taking care of both of them. They loved you as if you were their own. And whether anyone wants to admit it or not — you were the one who was there with them every single day. Thank you for all you did.

Sincerely,

Jacqueline

Taking a seat at the kitchen table I decided it was the proper thing to do to write back to her and thank her for her kind words. And to also thank her for using her own judgment on the situation instead of listening to her brother's advice. So, pulling out my paper, pen, and envelope I did just that.

Dear Jacqueline,

I received your letter and I am truly touched by your belief in me. It brings tears to my eyes. All along I thought I would be fighting this battle alone. Finally getting to tell my side to someone has me wanting to shout that I didn't do it. In fact, I didn't do anything wrong. Sure, your brothers have a right not to trust me – the words of a total stranger – as do you but I would have never hurt them in any way. I loved them like family and they were an important part of my life – especially your dad. Oh, how I wish you would've come to see them sooner.

The evidence report came back from California just earlier today and it came as no surprise to me when they said nothing matched and just like that I was released as if nothing had ever happened. While the two police officers were kind enough to drive me home, I could see everyone outside the window watching me as we drove past them. I could sense they were judging me as if I were guilty of something but I am innocent.

Lately, it seems everything is falling apart. First the bookstore, then your parents, and now my tarnished reputation. Oh, listen to me rambling on about my problems when you have just lost both of your parents. Gosh, I'm so sorry. I just feel so lost without them and without a job. I just don't know what I'll do now. I will say some prayers for you and your brothers to help heal your pain through this time.

Sincerely,

Abriana

P.S. I very much appreciate you bailing me out of jail. I honestly cannot thank you enough and one day I will repay you. Speaking of which, how much do I owe you for such a kind gesture?

Soon after I finished sealing the envelope of the letter, I heard a light knock at the front door. Drying my eyes, I tried to compose myself as best I could for whoever was on the porch.

Looking out the window I found a man I did not recognize. His height was rather short, circling his eyes were a thick pair of glasses sitting on a baby face. He was wearing an unwrinkled suit and gripping a briefcase tightly in his left hand.

"Good afternoon, ma'am," the man said removing his hat to show off his greasy yet receding hairline.

"It's close to evening by now sir...what is the reason for this late business call?" I asked in response barely holding the door open. I positioned my body weight against the door as I clutched the knob harshly. I rested my right foot against the door frame while the left I kept against the corner of the door itself in case I needed the leverage to try and get the door shut against him in a struggle.

I felt vulnerable without the protection of Benson but even worse without a weapon. Somehow before I owned the gun, I knew I was safe as long as Benson was there. Although he was up in age no one messed with him. He had a violent background and a short temper that a lot of people around here knew about so no one would dare mess with him because of the reputation he still held to the day.

"Ah – so it is ma'am," he said almost nervously. "My name is Briar Woodson and I work with Gail Masseoto. She is the assigned realtor for this property however my job is to handle all the preparations for the house to be put on the market for sale. Would you mind terribly if I came in so I could make some notes about the inside of the home? I apologize for the time of day but I did call earlier and no one seemed to pick up."

"Do you have identification? I would like to see the proof that you are who you say you are before I let you in." At a time like this, I couldn't trust just anyone since it was obvious someone was trying to harm me. Upon showing me his license and business card, I let him enter. "And I'm sorry who exactly hired you?"

"Oliver. The youngest son of the late owners of this house," he said as he looked around the foyer before setting his briefcase down. "May I?" I watched as he gestured to the closet door to him.

"You may," I said coldly. "If you'll excuse me, I will leave you to it. I have some business to conduct on my own." Turning my back to him before he spoke again, I headed for the kitchen to make myself a sandwich. My stomach was burning

106

and it reminded me that I hadn't eaten anything substantial today.

As I turned the corner to head into the kitchen, I saw that Mr. Woodson had draped his coat over his briefcase and balanced his hat on top of that. In his hand, he held a notebook, and without looking up from he was taking notes at a high speed.

The time it took me to make and almost finish eating my sandwich was the exact time Mr. Woodson entered the kitchen to begin his assessment of that room. I watched as he began opening cabinets and inspecting the contents inside. Stopping occasionally to write something down in his notebook. He pulled a tape measure from his back pocket and began his measurements inside the room.

"So, when is the house expected to be up for sale?" I asked him while continuing to watch his every move.

"Oliver strongly suggested it be done on or before the end of the week," he said without looking over at me.

"Do you expect it to be a quick sale?" I asked him curiously, trying my best to hide my disappointment as the lump in my throat began to swell.

"I do. This house is in a very sought-after location – it's considered to be in the city without being in the hustle of the city, very prime indeed. It doesn't require much outside maintenance and inside so far has been impressively taken care of considering its age and the ages of the homeowners. Plus, the market is quite competitive right now, there are a lot of buyers and not a lot of available houses. We shouldn't have a problem selling even over the asking price." He stared at me briefly after his explanation before giving me a quick sympathetic smile and looking away to continue with his duties.

"What is the asking price?" I asked even though I knew I wouldn't be able to afford it and even if I did, they probably wouldn't agree to me buying it.

Wiping the invisible sweat from his forehead he glanced over in my direction before licking his finger to flip to the next page of his notebook. "Ma'am–"

"My name is Abriana."

"Miss Abriana, I'm sorry I can't disclose that information to you. Oliver was very specific on some details and in my personal opinion I just don't think you need to concern yourself with the cost of the house."

"I'm afraid I don't understand Mr. Woodson. From your previous conversation, it seemed apparent to me that your job is to sell homes or at least help in making sure Gail sells this home. What connection am I missing?"

"I don't know how to say this without sounding rude and I apologize ahead of time for that but you are considered a conflict of interest in this matter. Therefore, you have been deemed someone that the seller does not wish to enter an agreement with concerning selling this house. Basically, what I'm trying to say is that they will never agree to sell the house to you." He made a few more quick notes before walking past me and out into the hallway.

"And what about all the belongings inside?" I asked following him to the banister as he began to climb the steps.

"To my knowledge, I was told everything will be sold with the house and it will be up to the new owners to do with the items whatever they please."

I left it at that so that he may continue with his audit of the house. Close to four hours had passed before he finished – being sure not to forget his belongings on the way out even though his head was still consumed with his written words in the notebook.

109

Chapter XI

Unchanged

Mr. Woodson was right – the house did sell quickly. Within a week of it being advertised many families came to take a tour and this started a bidding war when multiple individuals were not willing to give it up to one another so easily. To my knowledge through brief conversations with Gail and Briar, it seemed that Oliver accepted the offer that came in once one family had finally decided to give up. I was expected to be out in a month so that the new owners could move in.

The day they told me the news I started packing. I would need every bit of time to prepare and not because I had a lot to pack – I didn't – but because it would take me time to look for where I would be staying.

Fast Forward:

"I bet you never thought you'd be back here again," a woman's voice said to me from behind.

"I can't thank you enough for allowing me to move back in here Giorgia. I am truly grateful for all of you." Setting the last box on the floor I gave her a tight hug before she departed.

"Noon tomorrow?" I asked her as she headed out the door.

"We will see you then," she said smiling at me before closing the door.

I rubbed the rusted tin cookie jar between the palms of my hands which had remained on the counter untouched since I had last placed it there. Inside, I found the money I had left in there for them – it too was untouched but there was something that was not there before – a small piece of paper shoved down to the bottom, smashed, and crinkled. *For if you shall ever return.* Is what it read in Nannina's handwriting, hugging it closely I buried the cookie jar deep in the back of the kitchen cabinet where I had first found it.

For the remainder of the night, I unpacked as much as I could to help tire me out so I could fall asleep. By the end of the night, I was fairly satisfied with how much I had gotten accomplished. Settling down on my kitchen stool I broke open a bottle of wine as I looked off in the distance to the picture of Benson and Denise I had hanging on my wall. I had downed half the bottle to drown my sorrows before I decided it was finally time to head off to bed.

"Ero molto triste di sentire parlare di Denise e Benson. Mi dispiace per la tua perdita," Nannina said to me upon entering the kitchen.

111

"Thank you Nannina," I said, giving her a warm embrace for sharing her sympathy during my recent loss.

"This will sound selfish but I'm so happy you're back home with us," she said cupping my face like a child with her cold hands. They smelled of dough and tomato sauce, making me feel like I was exactly where I should be.

"Hi!" a warm voice enthusiastically shrieked in my direction. "I'm Claire!"

"Claire was the new you…before you returned," Giorgia said with a chuckle.

"Può pensare quello che vuole, ma non potrebbe mai sostituirti," Nannina said to me with a wink as she passed by me to finish her preparations.

I laughed as Giorgia shook her head at her before looking back to me and rolling her eyes, "As you can see little has changed around here." She cleared her throat before shooting a glare at Nannina to behave herself.

An exaggerated huff came from behind me which I assumed stemmed from Nannina.

"What did she say, Giorgia?" Claire asked, still in her chipper mood.

"She said you are a hard worker just like Abriana," her eyes quickly darting to mine and back to Claires. "So," Giorgia clapped her hands together

112

loudly to abruptly change the subject before any more lying was deemed necessary. "Where is it that you would like to be at my dear...podium or tables?"

"Tables please," I said with only a brief hesitation.

Fast Forward:

Before long a month had passed and with it giving me enough time to settle back into my apartment and my once familiar job. Most of my mornings before work and evenings after I would spend unpacking to get rid of every item I didn't need, reminiscing through old memories and crying along the way.

It was a warmer than usual Tuesday coming out of spring when I returned to work for the week. The Greco's had been kind enough to give me a long weekend off – including Monday – since I was needed through the following weekend due to a staffing issue. Arriving at work fifteen minutes before my shift I went to the kitchen to check on Nannina being sure to say hi to Claire on the way through so she didn't think I was upset with her about who knows what. During the trip to the kitchen, a man caught my attention. He was middle height, middle age, and had a smooth-shaven baby face. He had dark hair that swooped and bright blue eyes that were enough to make you think you were getting lost in a view of the ocean.

"Hi," he said in a smooth voice as I scooted past him. He held a bright smile on his face with dimples deep enough to hold an unripened blueberry. By the look of him, I knew he was trouble and not to waste my time looking twice. But he was a mix between Danny and Nicholas. And something about that drew me to him just as something warned me to steer clear.

"Hello," I said sweetly. Venturing into the kitchen I was informed that Nannina was taking the day off to rest.

"WHO is the hunk?" Claire asked practically jumping out of her skin as she watched him from the kitchen door.

I decided not to watch her as I replied. And I highly doubted her *love at first sight* eyes would be going away anytime soon. "Uh…I don't know. I haven't been back long enough to tell you if he is a regular or not. Unless maybe you know?"

"I have NEVER seen THAT creature before," she said in a serious way.

To this, I busted into laughter. "He is a MAN not a piece of meat or a God for that matter."

"He is to me," she whispered. Whether her comment was meant for me to hear I'll never know but my sharp hearing regrettably caught it away.

The weeks and months carried on and throughout that time Claire's hunk religiously stopped in every week on the same day like clockwork. But he never graced us with his presence more than once in a seven-day stretch. I don't think he could've overstayed his welcome if he tried. If Claire had it her way, she'd want him to come in every day. His cologne was strong in an almost overpowering way but it had a nice fragrance.

During this time, we became acquaintances through small talk and occasionally having his table. I preferred to stay clear of him and keep as much distance as I could – wanting very much not to converse with him regularly but he kept on pursuing me and since he was a customer I had to try to be as professionally accommodating as I could be. Through our brief discussions, I learned that his name was Denver and he was relatively new to the area. Sadly, I had heard a similar story to his before.

"Can I interest you in going to dinner with me one day this weekend?" he randomly asked on his usual Thursday schedule.

"I–I'm sorry but no. I don't even know you," I said listening to the little voice inside my head that was throwing red flags at me.

"Yes, I know but isn't that how you get to know someone that you don't? By spending time with them and going out on dates?" he asked in his gentlemanly tone. "Besides it's not like we are *complete* strangers. I do consider myself a regular customer here and I think the rest of the employees would agree.

"Maybe that's true but I am just not interested," I said turning my back on him and walking away.

"Not even if we eat here?" he asked innocently.

"Eat here?" I asked, turning around to face him. "Now why would you want to do a thing like that?" I curiously cocked my head to the side while staring at him wide-eyed.

"To help make you more comfortable of course. I don't mind it at all. The food here is good and I know the service is exceptional. In fact, we could eat here as many times as it takes."

I appreciated his thoughtful consideration but I still didn't know if it was the right thing to do. Especially since Claire was simply head over heels – pining for the man. What would she think of me if I did that? She would think I was doing it to her on purpose – to hurt her or *worse* to steal her man –

116

which couldn't be further from the truth. I couldn't think of her taking it any other way than that especially since I knew she liked him enormously.

"That's incredibly generous but my answer is still no," I said politely with a small smile. I could feel Claire's eyes digging into my back. She was basically breathing down my neck from where she stood and I wanted nothing more than to remove myself from the situation as quickly as I possibly could.

Fast Forward:

"Hey doll!" an unfamiliar man's voice shouted after me late one night as I was locking up the restaurant. Giorgia had left early as she was feeling under the weather and so did Mr. Greco to get home at a decent hour to take care of her. I had insisted that Nannina not wait for me and for her to leave before dark set in, allowing me to close up the restaurant on my own.

"I'm sorry, I'm not the *doll* you speak of, you must have me confused with someone else. I've *never* seen you *before* in my life," I said to him sternly. The man appeared to be completely intoxicated and could barely keep his balance.

"You're right about that!" he said forcing a brown paper bag into the air, that held the contents of a liquor bottle by its obvious shape. "You're an angel." He bowed mockingly.

"I don't think so…" I said turning quickly from him and heading towards the next door to get to my apartment.

Suddenly I felt a sharp tug on my purse strap, pulling me back slightly just before I reached the door. "On second thought maybe you're right about that – maybe you're not an angel after all. Don't you know…it's rude to leave without saying goodbye," he said agitated with my decision. I tried my best to shake it out of his grip before the thought of his hands could have a chance to slither around my body.

But all I heard next was the hammer of a gun being cocked before I turned around. Holding my hands up I lifted my arms to the air slowly, raising them above my head. "All I have is in my purse – just take it and leave." Only when I faced him head-on did I see what was really happening.

"Leave the lady *alone* and I won't put a *bullet* in your head." Looking past the drunken fool who was attempting to mug me I saw Denver standing behind the attacker. He had one arm around his neck while the other was holding a gun to his temple. "Say that

118

you understand what I'm telling you." I noticed that he spoke slowly so that the befuddled man could follow along with the words he was saying to him.

"I…under…stand…" the man said between drunken breaths.

He spun the man around after releasing him, making him dance about completely unbalanced. When the man was finally able to stand straight enough to look him in the eye Denver said, "Now leave here and if you should ever return, I won't hesitate to pull the trigger."

Allowing myself to catch my breath, I stayed still – plastered to the outside of the door. "Wha– what are you doing here?" I asked.

"It's Thursday," he said confused by the question.

"It is…" I said trailing off into thought.

"Wow, I don't know if it's hurt that I'm feeling knowing you didn't even notice that I hadn't come in today." His playful smile quickly faded once he realized I wasn't in the best of moods.

"It had been a long day…" I said, watching him put his gun away. Looking down at my purse I nervously tugged on the stretched strap. "I don't know how I'll ever repay you for what you did Denver. Thank you…for saving me."

"No need. I'm just glad I was later than usual to stop by the restaurant. You might not have been that lucky if I hadn't been running late. I didn't know what time the restaurant was open until and I figured I might as well take a trip passed."

"Well, I'm certainly glad you did," I said with tears forming in my eyes.

A slow smile had begun to form on his face once more before dissolving away entirely upon reading the current state of my body language. "Me too...and there's no need to get emotional Abriana. You're safe...when I'm around at least." He smiled sincerely but I looked right through him as if he were a ghost, still in shock at what had just happened. "Now the only thing left to do is for you to agree to go to dinner with me. I'll accept that as payment for tonight."

To this, I laughed – knowing very well that he was both partially serious and partially joking. But if it came down to one over the other – I knew which one he would favor.

Chapter XII

Blossom

Seeing as my presence was requested by Denver and he didn't seem to trust me not to stand him up – our dinner followed late one evening at the Greco's once everyone else had left for the night – including the staff, more importantly including Claire. I had agreed to go on *one* date with him to repay him for saving my life.

"What did you order?" I asked calling to Denver from the table as I laid out the plates and silverware for our dinner. Apparently, he had done that part all on his own, not allowing me to take part in it – even in the slightest.

"Pizza!" he said enthusiastically, arriving with it on a large pan and a pizza cutter.

"Pizza?" I repeated almost disappointed. "That's certainly an interesting choice for a date."

"I would've said *simple* but I'll take *interesting* as a compliment," he said with a laugh. "Besides it's not about the food as it is about the conversation and…connection."

I began choking on my wine as his lips mouthed the word *connection*. "I'm sorry to disappoint you Denver but there is *no* connection."

"You don't know that yet…it's too early to tell at this point," he said with confidence.

He was either crazy or blind to what was really going on here which was nothing. Sure, he was an attractive man – and most women would have agreed with me on the subject but that's as far as it went for me. He just *looked* good and that was the extent of it.

"Plain or mushrooms?" he asked as a way of changing the subject.

But I wasn't going to be strayed away from questioning him that easily. "Plain…and why did you want to do dinner with me anyway?"

I watched as he cut the pizza into perfectly sized pieces – like he had done this all his life. He didn't hesitate when he ran the blade of the cutter at the angle he wanted. Watching his hands, I could see that he didn't feel the need to apply an over amount of pressure while doing it either – which was a skill that most customers hadn't acquired while cutting most of their meals.

"Not to be too obnoxious but I was very much attracted to you the first time I laid eyes on you. And I don't know…I guess it's just one of those things that I wanted to get to know more about you. Call it a feeling or whatnot but…I can't really explain it any better than that." His face continued to blush while he attempted to explain the reasoning to me.

"Well then here's to it being just *one of those things*," I said holding my glass of wine high for him to tap mine.

"Cheers," he said with a wide smile. Taking a long gulp of the wine he got back to work with the final touches of cutting the pizza before serving the both of us.

We talked for what seemed like hours but really it was a lot longer than that. I had lost track of time when he began to open the third bottle of wine. Denver was a kind man with a listening ear and mature advice. Through his own stories, it was easy to see that he too had ghosts from his past – a time when he wasn't pleased with himself. But then again, we all did.

I wasn't sure if it was the wine or me just feeling comfortable with opening up and being vulnerable with someone again but I told him my life story as he had so easily shared his. I even told him the parts that were difficult to talk about – Danny, our unborn child, and of course Nicholas.

Selfish and ruthless were the two words that Denver used to describe what Nicholas had done. Especially the stunts he pulled during his time as Gabriele.

"I have to say that is quite unheard of – it has to be," he said with a light laugh. "But from the depths of my body, I am sorry that all happened to you. That's absolutely horrible. You endured more than most, I am sure. You are a strong woman, don't ever forget that, and don't ever doubt that. I am truly amazed by you. I have to say I didn't expect to *hear* all this tonight."

Laughing at the silliness of it I said, "And I didn't expect to *share* all of this tonight."

"So…whatever happened to dear old Gabriele or shall we call him Nicholas?" he asked, tossing back a mouthful of wine.

The unexpected question threw me into a whirlwind. My body froze in an instant. My head became fuzzy as if the wine was beginning to catch up with me. All of a sudden it seemed I couldn't collect my thoughts quick enough to answer the question. But I had to be careful not to answer too quickly and look guilty of…something. "I uhh…I actually don't know what became of him…he just sort of…disappeared out of my life. And I haven't heard from him since – thankfully."

I wasn't sure why I felt the need to lie. I should've just told him the truth as everyone else had known it to keep the story consistent.

"Well, let us cheers to that too then!" Clanging our glasses together I looked off in the distance to get away from his longing eyes. "I'm glad you feel comfortable enough to share these things with me Abriana. It seems like you obviously needed to get all this off your chest." He sipped his wine slowly as he continued to watch me. "And I can't tell you how long it's been since I've had a real conversation with a woman – talking about deep subjects. It feels really good actually."

Ignoring his feelings, I couldn't help but wonder why he thought that. "How did you know that?" I asked anxiously. "That I needed to get some things off my chest – as you put it?"

"I could tell. Soon after you finished you let out a breath that seemed to be finally escaping from your lips. It just looked like you had been holding all that in for a long time. I'm sorry – do forgive me – it appears my parents both being doctors rubbed off on me more than I'd like to admit at times. I seem to be pretty decent at reading people, studying them, analyzing them – helping them even at times."

I reached for the bottle to refill my wine glass for the fiftieth time tonight but not before he grabbed it and poured it for me. "They must be quite proud of you Denver."

"Yes, I dare say they are," he said laughing. I didn't understand the inside joke but he did – assuming it was just a family thing I shrugged it off. "Do you dance Abriana?"

Clearing my throat, I began to cough on the remaining wine that had gotten lodged in my windpipe. "Oh, heavens no! I haven't danced since Nic–Gabriele and I got married."

Rushing around the table he grabbed both of my arms and held them completely straight – high above my head. "This is a technique my parents would use on me when I was a child. Not that you're a child of course but it helps when a liquid goes down the wrong pipe like this. Holding both of your arms high above your head as such helps to open your diaphragm allowing you to breathe easier and choke less," he said matter-of-factly with a sweet giggle.

"Thank you, Denver," I said in admiration as the coughing slowly but surely began to lessen.

"How about that dance before we part ways for the night?" His blue eyes were drowning mine.

Dropping our gaze, I stared at my freshly filled wine glass. "It's getting late. We should probably both head home."

"Just one dance…it won't kill you or harm me," he said in a persuading manner. Before I could protest again, he had me by the hand and was pulling me up from the chair. He twirled me around only once thankfully since the room was beginning to spin already on its own. He moved so naturally like his body was made for this. I felt like we were drifting on a cloud or better yet I was standing on his feet and he was doing all the dancing. We floated as he guided me through the open space of the dining room.

"I had fun tonight," I said to him standing inside my apartment. "And thank you for walking me up the stairs."

"It was the least I could do considering we are both a little tipsier than I thought we'd be." His smile was infectious and those dimples made him almost irresistible. "I had fun too maybe we could do this again sometime."

"I'd like that," I blurted out on accident. "Sorry, that's the wine…I think."

"Well, at least the wine likes me enough to approve of a next time…" He held hope in his eyes but for what I didn't know. "Goodnight Abriana." With a swift move, he gave me a small peck on the cheek before showing himself out.

The next morning on my way down the stairs I noticed my mailbox looking a little fuller than normal. There was the usual junk mail in there, bills of course, and a letter from Jacqueline.

Dear Abriana,

Please know that you are never alone in your battles. I know at times it may seem that way but you are not. You are incredibly strong and it is because of this that you have survived all that has happened to you. Don't ever let that light inside of you burn out. Keep that flame lit — that fire burning. That is wonderful news about the findings from the evidence report — wonderful for you but not so much for the murders. I have since told my brothers of your innocence; they still seem skeptical but with time I'm sure they too will come around. Especially when the police actually arrest the right person. And please don't apologize for being human we all have these hard times where we wish we had someone to talk to about them. I am probably the closest one who knows the reality of what's going on right now better than anyone. Don't ever feel like a bother when you need to talk, I am here to listen anytime you need me — consider me simply a pen stroke away. Also, I want to end this letter by saying I regret to inform you that — as much as I wish to take credit for it, I cannot — it was neither myself nor my brothers that posted your bail to be released. But I am so incredibly happy to hear that someone did. Looks like you have a guardian angel on your side over there. Enclosed you should find a check addressed to you from me. This was the money received from the insurance company for the arson. It looks to be enough to rebuild the bookstore since he owned the building if that were to be something you'd ever be interested in. As I have mentioned before I never wanted anything from my father and I still don't. Please do with the money what you wish.

Sincerely,

Jacqueline

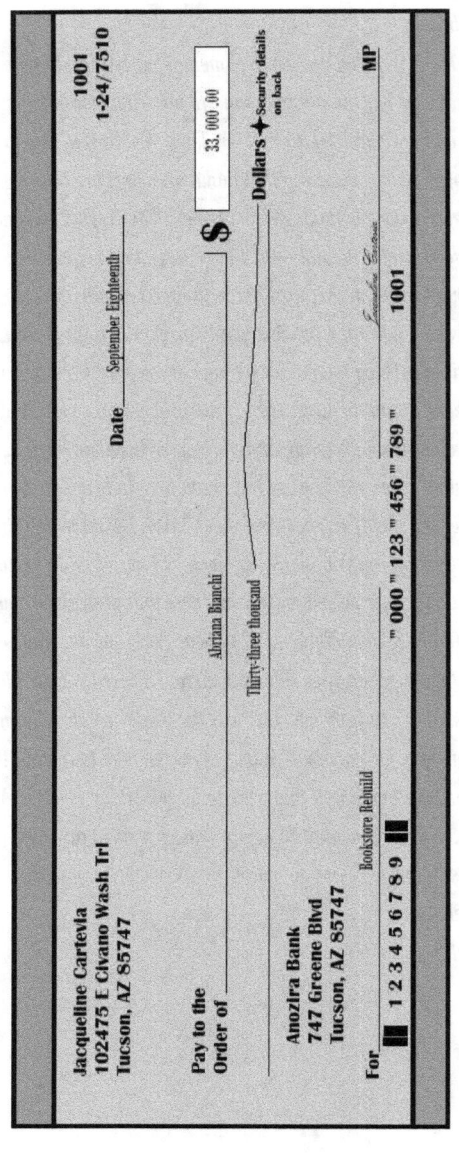

Jacqueline Cartevia
102475 E Civano Wash Trl
Tucson, AZ 85747

1001
1-24/7510

Date _____ September Eighteenth _____

Pay to the
Order of _____ Adriana Bianchi _____ $ | 33,000.00 |

Thirty-three thousand _____ Dollars → Security details on back

Anozira Bank
747 Greene Blvd
Tucson, AZ 85747

Jacqueline Cartevia

For _____ Bookstore Rebuild _____   1001

" 000 " 123 " 456 " 789 "   MP

█ 1 2 3 4 5 6 7 8 9 █

130

What? If Jacqueline didn't bail me out...then who did? Even after arriving at work and starting with my usual duties I still couldn't concentrate. I couldn't get this out of my mind.

"Hey! These came for you earlier...must've been one *hell* of a night," Claire said with a huff.

Confused I looked to see what she was talking about. A large vase filled with a dozen of roses stood vibrantly on the counter. The mix of red petals and green leaves looked like Christmas itself stuffed in a glass container. I smiled at the sight of them.

"Who's the note from?" she asked anxiously pointing at it while my head was buried in the flowers to smell their sweet scent.

Thanks again –
Had a lot of fun.
– D

Rereading the card two times over I began to remember bits of pieces of what happened last night. "Oh, these are just from a friend," I said trying my best to brush it off.

"That's some *friend*," she said bending one of the rose's heads back before letting it go, making it spring forward.

I was beginning to wonder if someone had told Claire that it was Denver, whom I had dinner with last night. She was acting very strange today.

"Table four requests your presence my dear," Giorgia whispered as she walked past me, pulling me from my thoughts.

Chapter XIII

Company

"How can I help y–you...YOU? What are you doing here?" I asked, frantically looking around at the people staring as I lowered my voice.

"Alright, alright – calm down sugar I already know how excited you are to see me. I can tell," Matteo said with a smile and a toothpick hanging out of the corner of his mouth.

"Have you been chewing on the same one all this time because if so, you might want to consider changing," I said, slamming down the open container of fresh toothpicks as I motioned to the one in between his teeth.

"You know, I always admired your sense of humor. That so-called spark in you really keeps me feeling alive! Keeps me on my toes. WOO-HEE!"

"Keep your voice DOWN! We are in a place of business better known as my boss's establishment and you aren't a *wild* animal!"

"Sugar...you have no idea *what* I am," he said with a disturbing laugh.

"What are you doing here anyway?" I said, lining the table with fresh silverware and menus.

"Well, why do *you* think I'm here? I do enjoy getting your perspective on these things, nowadays."

"I have *no* idea – none in the slightest! That's why I'm asking!" I said in a hushed but aggravated tone. "And where's your *sidekick*? Is he in the bathroom or something?"

"Funny you should mention Antonio. It's crazy how much of a *coincidence* everything just *seems* to be with you." He continued to stare at me as if I already knew what was really going on.

I looked back and forth between both of his eyes for a minute or two before answering, completely confused by his attendance here today. "Huh?"

"Why don't you uh…take a seat. I'll talk to your boss if they come over and explain the…*situation.*"

I didn't like the sound of that at all. Had there been a break in the case suddenly? Was this the moment I had been waiting for? He was going to tell me he had found the killer and arrested them.

"My buddy old pal seemed to disappear after the interrogation, actually soon after your release if I'm recalling everything right. You wouldn't know anything about that now, would you?" he asked leaning over the table towards me.

"Most certainly NOT!" I said in an outrage.

"No need to get defensive Abriana. You must be careful with that now; some men of the law would take that kind of a reaction as guiltiness."

"Guilty of what? This is *ridiculous* Matteo. I should report the both of you for harassment."

"Ooo–honey now that's a tough one because the law is always right above the common folk. The badge helps with that. And trust me, if there's one thing you don't want to do is go against the badge." He had a malicious smile on his face as if he had already won – little did he know the battle hadn't even begun yet. And you can't claim a victory over an action that didn't happen.

"So, are you trying to say Antonio had something to do with Benson's murder?" I glared at him over the table, crossing my arms tight against my chest.

"Now that is a strong allegation, Miss Abriana. I wonder, how in the world do you come up with such ideas?"

"I don't know what you want from me Matteo," I said, slowly coming to a stand. "But it sounded to me like you wanted me to fit the puzzle pieces together that you gave me. So, unless you have something else…something *important* for me, then I suggest you let me get back to doing my job."

"Phew – you are a pistol girl," he whispered as I backed away from him and headed towards the counter.

Giorgia replaced my services with another one of the waitresses to take care of Matteo – for this, I was eternally grateful.

"Well, you ladies all have a good day," he announced as he pounded his fist down on the front counter. But just before he left, he made sure to make eye contact with me. "I'll be seeing you around Miss Abriana."

Not long after the doorbell rang, I fled for the outside – having one more question to ask Matteo before he left. "HEY!" I yelled approaching his vehicle. "How did you even know where I was anyway?"

At this, he chuckled. "I have my sources. Thanks for the new toothpick." Slamming the car door, he sped off in the opposite direction of the restaurant and my apartment.

The rest of the day I was in a fog. All I could think about was Antonio. If he had killed Benson then that would mean it was an inside job – being covered up by the police force and their dirty cops. And if that was the case then Matteo had to be corrupt too because there was no way his partner could be bad and he wasn't, right? Even after all that it still came down to one question – why murder Benson? He didn't have anything to do with anything, he was clean. *The only thing he was guilty of was being a grumpy, old man for goodness sake.*

Fast Forward:

"Did you like the flowers I sent earlier in the week?" Denver whispered to me since Claire had just walked by.

"I did, thank you," I said coldly as I finished collecting the plates from the table next to his.

"Okay…I can tell something is wrong. What is it – what happened?" The intuitive side of him had kicked in.

"I had a visit from Matteo this week. The conversation we had…has left me feeling unsettled I guess you could say."

"Was there any new news on Benson?" he said taking a bite of his sandwich.

"No, there wasn't. In fact, it would seem he didn't come down here because of Benson at all. He came down here to see if I had seen or heard from his partner, Antonio."

"The aggressor? Maybe he's somehow involved. But why would you have any contact with him?" he asked curiously.

"Your guess is as good as mine," I said putting the rest of the silverware on the tray and carrying it off to the kitchen to be cleaned.

"I know a place where we can blow off some steam from the long week if you're interested," Denver proposed as I locked up the restaurant.

"Don't you have work tomorrow? How are you going to be up all hours of the night if you have to get up early?"

"Actually, I took tomorrow off. It's been a stressful four days, to say the least, and I didn't think I could do a fifth. A long weekend will do me some good. Aren't you off tomorrow too?"

"Yeah, I am, how did you know that?" I asked surprised.

"I overheard Claire telling you to enjoy your extra days off." He laughed at my seriousness.

"I don't know Denver. I'm really tired, I think I just want to head off to bed."

"Come on Abriana, we won't stay out too late, promise." He stuck out his pinky finger to me as if we were agreeing on something unbreakable.

"Ugh…" I groaned as I rolled my eyes at him. "Fine! But only *one* hour, okay?"

I watched as his feet left the ground in excitement. "You're the boss. I'll take what I can get."

"Where *are* we?" I asked as I choked on clouds of smoke and the heavy smell of liquor. The air around us was so polluted we might as well have been outside walking through fog. I was beginning to feel as if I was in a horror movie – when humans turned to zombies – with all the red eyes, dry mouths, and drooling we had passed on the way through.

I didn't belong here and I could feel it. Every nerve in my body screamed it. My skin tingled and not in a good way. It was tight and tense with anxiety. This was by far my dumbest idea. I should've just gone home like I wanted to. Why did I let him talk me into this?

"It's an underground club for gambling – kept under tight wraps," he said excitedly as he pulled through the dance floor.

"This doesn't look like gambling to me," I said walking past women dancing on poles and the tops of tables. Men wearing wedding rings rained money on some while others tucked bills into whatever opening they could. Drunken women clung to the sides of their chairs or laid face down on the bar's countertop, too far gone to keep their heads up any longer.

"This is the nightclub – the gambling section is through here," he said guiding me the rest of the way.

When we reached a heavily bolted red door two men stood side by side guarding it. Denver flashed a special token at them in the shape of a coin. They nodded their heads at him and motioned towards the door as they stepped aside for us to walk between them. They eyed me suspiciously, no doubt wondering what I was doing here. And I was still left to think the same. But it wasn't too late I could still turn around and leave now.

"Hey Den–"

"One second Abriana." He pounded on the door a beat I had never heard before. Within seconds a small rectangular window slid open, revealing a man that looked similar to Popeye the sailor man. Denver said something that sounded like it was in a different language. Suddenly the window slid shut again with a slam and I heard bolts being unlocked.

"Denver I'm sorry. I've changed my mind; can you take me home please?"

"Awe come now Abriana – we are so close. It's just right behind this door," he said cupping my face. "Remember we needed to blow off some steam?" Denver put his hand on the door and softly rubbed it back and forth. "Well, as soon as this door opens that's what we are going to do. I swear you'll be glad you came. By the end of the night, you'll be thanking me. It's going to be so much fun!"

I was apprehensive from the start and even more so now yet I still followed him through the red metal door of death. It slammed behind me making me jump. Now on the other side, I could see why it took so long to open because of how many locks the Popeye lookalike was going through and fixing. What was so important that had to be locked away back here?

"Ta-da! Here we are!" Denver announced with his arms spread wide to display the room. "Pick which table you want to play at and I'll pay tonight it's my treat!"

"Pay? Wait...we are playing for money? Like cash under the table – money?" I could feel my eyes bugging out of my head at the illegalness going on in here.

"That's right! That's what gambling is all about – winning and losing money. Although you always hope you win more than you lose." He laughed in a strange way I had never heard before.

I now saw why this place was kept locked up so tightly. Between this – which was isn't legal – and all the people in here cutting and taking lines on some card tables – whoever ran this operation would most definitely go to jail.

When I didn't answer Denver walked me over to the table where a man was holding a handful of cards shuffling them between their fingers while others threw theirs into a pile towards the middle with a piss-poor attitude. "I'll be right back I'm going to get a drink; do you want water?"

"Yes please – definitely a water," I said shaking my head.

"Gotcha I'll be right back! Don't deal her in yet until I get back," he told the man standing in the middle of the table.

Within a few minutes, Denver returned with our drinks. I chugged the water at a tremendous speed as I was parched from our adventure thus far.

"Deal us in." Once the dealer had gotten caught up with what was happening around the table, he began throwing cards in Denver's direction. Handing me the cards he said, "Okay listen very carefully. I'm going to explain the rules and what we have to do in this game. So, what you're going to do is–"

Suddenly there was a ringing in my ears – it kept getting louder and louder until I couldn't hear anything he or anyone was saying. I couldn't hear the ice cubes clanging in the glasses around me as people drank their liquor. I couldn't hear the woman shamelessly laughing at jokes that weren't funny. I couldn't even hear Denver as he whispered in my ears. All there was, was a constant ringing.

The dealer's head began to shift in shape and size as if he were standing in front of a funhouse mirror. Suddenly I felt as if I was that mirror. Then the room began to spin – swirling around me and it didn't stop. I could feel myself drifting, falling away from here. I was losing my balance and beginning to sway. The last thing I remember before my eyes rolled into the back of my head was seeing Gabriele's face off in the far distance of the room and me reaching my hand in that direction – then everything went black.

"Okay…time to go. I got you," I could hear a voice that sounded like Denver's say as my body was hoisted up. I could hear the sound of vomiting. I could feel my mouth opening and closing and something spraying out of it but I couldn't get my eyes to open. The unconsciously conscious vomiting continued until I couldn't remember if I was awake or asleep anymore.

Chapter XIV

Unwelcome

"Abriana…" I heard a voice call my name off in the distance. I could feel my body shaking slightly, swaying back and forth. "Abriana, come on now, wake up! Open your eyes Abriana!"

When my lids did lift themselves, I saw that it was daylight. I was in a fog, confused, and drained. I held my hand up to shield my face from the brightness of the sun. By the position of it shining through the window, I guessed it was noon or almost.

"Ooo– sorry! I'll shut those!" a familiar voice said. Once the blinds were pulled to block out the rays, I could see that it was Denver in my apartment.

"Wha–what are you doing here?" I asked shakily trying to prop myself up on my elbows.

"Oh, here let me help you!" he said sweetly as he reached for me to try to sit me up.

"Don't TOUCH me!" I partially shouted at him.

"Huh?" He looked completely astounded that I was yelling at him.

"You – you drugged me last night!" I said louder, fighting to find my voice.

"I did WHAT? Come on Abriana, don't be ridiculous!"

"Well, then how do you explain what happened to me huh? You go to get me water and come back and that's all I had and suddenly I'm blacking out! WHY DID YOU DO IT? HOW COULD YOU?"

"Abriana I—"

"STOP LIEING DENVER!" I waited for him to speak. To admit that he did it and why but he fell silent and continued to stare at me, breathing heavily like an animal. Like a predator getting ready to pounce on its prey. "You are no longer welcome here. Get out."

"What? This is *ridiculous* Abriana, I didn't—"

"GET OUT OF MY APARTMENT! Or I *will* call the police!"

Raising his hands in silence as if he was already tried as guilty, he slithered away and out the door. I cried for hours. The first reason is that this was someone I was really beginning to trust, really beginning to get close to. Someone that I had considered a friend had done something like this to me. Betrayal traveled through my bloodstream like shards of glass – it hurt, it burned.

How could I have been so wrong about him? But on the other hand, I hardly knew anything about him. He was just a regular, a customer. His life and mannerism outside the restaurant most likely did not reflect what we saw inside of it. I only knew the portions he had told me and who knew what was true and what was a lie.

The second reason I continued to cry – and this being the more important one – was I couldn't feel my legs, they were completely numb. When I tried to get out of bed I fell flat onto the floor. I was so weak I couldn't put my hands or arms out fast enough to lessen the blow. Hitting my face, nose, and busting my lip.

I laid there and cried for what seemed like hours before I felt I had the strength to try and drag myself to the kitchen, crawling on my belly. Using the chair to balance myself I pulled as hard as I could to get up. Once I was in the chair, I used my arms to try to make small jumps, hopping both myself and the seat over to the sink so I could get water in me. I could feel that I was completely dehydrated.

It wasn't until night when I regained feeling in my legs and feet to be able to get up and hobble around. I was so weak that I was incredibly unsteady so I had to use everything in my path as a crutch to make it to where I was trying to go.

After locking the apartment door and falling many times I made it to the bathtub so I could soak and get another good cry out of me. A knock came at the door that seemed like a mere minute later.

"Just a minute!" To my surprise however it was daylight again and I had fallen asleep in the bathtub. Slowly climbing out I made my way into the bedroom, getting dressed as quickly as possible.

Reaching the door, I found Mr. and Mrs. Greco in the most terrible of states.

Fast Forward:

"For as much as it has pleased Almighty God to take out of this world the soul of Nannina Greco, we, therefore, commit her body to the ground, earth to earth, ashes to ashes, dust to dust, looking for that blessed hope when the Lord Himself shall descend from heaven with a shout, with the voice of the archangel, and with the trump of God, and the dead in Christ shall rise first. Then we which are alive and remain shall be caught up together with them in the clouds to meet the Lord in the air, and so shall we ever be with the Lord, wherefore comfort ye one another with these words." These were the final sentences spoken at Nannina's gravesite the day she was buried.

It was a dark day, even the sky itself mourned with gloom. The clouds cried as I have never seen

147

before. They cried until the rain saturated the ground Nannina was put in. I stayed behind long after everyone had left. Even after the soil had been returned to its normal place, I stayed. I felt terrible leaving her there. I wept on top of the ground of her plot.

Oh, how I missed her already. There were so many things I wanted to say to her, that I never got the chance to and would never again. I will always be thankful for her – her kindness, wisdom, and love. She was gentle. I would always miss her. My heart had not yet healed over the loss of Benson and Denise and now Nannina.

The Greco's said they found her on the floor at their house. Apparently, she had fallen and hit her head. The coroner named it an accident. But for some reason, Giorgia didn't believe it. Either she was having just as much of a hard time accepting it as the rest of us or she suspected foul play. A note had been found crinkled up in Nannina's hand but it had to be sent away as evidence and it was too blood-soaked to be able to read the print. It appeared we would be relying on California once again.

After the burial, all the family and close friends headed to the restaurant to eat. It was what Nannina would've wanted. Greco's Garganelli meant so much to her. After all the restaurant was her life.

"Abriana..." Giorgia said when I arrived in her lost voice. "Please come to the kitchen, my husband and I would like to have a word."

We walked in silence past all those who were whispering and those that were looking off into space in disbelief of the day. The restaurant suddenly felt different. It felt less warm – I'd almost say cold. The colors on the walls were dull with sadness. Grief hung all around us.

"Please sit," Mr. Greco instructed as I entered the room motioning to one of the three bar stools set up by the island. "Abriana, the Mrs. and I have made the tough decision to close down the restaurant. This was Nannina's livelihood and with her being gone...it's just seeming like the right time to close the doors for good."

"What? No!" Instantly I was filled with even more despair.

"We aren't getting any younger dear," Giorgia said putting her hand on top of mine to help ease the pain. "At our age and with what just happened – it's time."

"We want to leave you with a portion of the profits acquired so far this year and this should keep you going for a good while. And you are more than

149

welcome to still live in the apartment." Mr. Greco's eyes were tired and filled with tears though he tried hard to keep them from falling.

"What if I told you I wanted to buy the restaurant from you? Would you let me take over running it and owning it?" I asked, thinking of the check Jacqueline sent me from the insurance for the bookstore. "I'll pay you thirty-three thousand dollars for it. That's all I have but it's worth it to me. I can't bear to see this place die out as the bookstore did." Just like that I couldn't hold it in anymore and began to cry.

"Make it fifteen and you got a deal," Mr. Greco said holding my other hand.

"What? Really?" I said excitedly.

"Really," he said wiping tears from his eyes. "Besides you'll need some cash on the side for emergencies just in case. "Greco's Garganelli is all yours and goes on to live another day!" The three of us hugged and cried, cherishing this moment.

Fast Forward:

"What has been up with you lately Abriana?" Claire asked nervously. "I'm worried about you!"

"Don't be, I'm fine. Hey, listen the business is paid off and I need a favor from you."

"Anything, you know that – name it!" she said enthusiastically.

"I want to add your name as co-owner of the restaurant with me. You know, just in case something would ever happen to me then it doesn't get lost or shut down permanently."

"If something happens to you? What are you talking about? Okay, now you're starting to scare me!"

"Just sign the damn papers please Claire!"

"Okay geez – you don't have to be so pushy."

"I'm leaving to file these and then I'm going to take the rest of the day off – will you be okay?" I was on edge and concerned. I wasn't quite sure why but I felt like I had the jitters even though I wasn't shaking.

"Yes, *boss* we will be fine here!" she said exaggeratedly as she threw her arms up in the air dramatically.

I rolled my eyes and snorted at her attitude before leaving the restaurant. *She'll be fine.*

"Abriana! It's always a pleasure to see you on our side of town!"

"Cut the crap Angelo – tell Emilio I'm here because I need some…" I said trailing off. I couldn't believe my life had come to this. Every morning and all through the night I fought hard against myself to stop but I just couldn't make myself do it. Ever since that night at the club and whatever Denver had put in my drink – it got me hooked in the worst of ways. And I needed it. Every day, all day I needed it. The craving was undeniable and it would not be ignored.

"You just had a gram yesterday? You can't tell me you hit that many times already."

I knew the only way to shut Angelo up was to put my money where his mouth was. So, I shoved a roll of cash in his face. "See this? I'm a paying customer and paying customers expect to get what they want. Now I told you to get Emilio! Give me what I want!"

"Geez – okay, calm down Abriana – you're bugging." He turned and headed inside the building, waiting patiently for me there while the guards outside patted me down to make sure I wasn't carrying.

By the time I had gotten back out to the car after talking to Emilio, my addiction had gotten worse. The craving had taken over and all I could think about was getting some of the drugs in my body to stop the incessant itch, the want, the need.

"Hey Abriana! What are you doing on this side of town?" a familiar voice yelled with concern.

Through my blurred vision, it looked to me like it was Denver walking toward my car. Firing up the engine I sped out of there almost running him over in the process. *I have to get back to my apartment, everything's starting to spin.*

Chapter XV

Confession

When I awoke, I was lying in a familiar-smelling room. Antiseptics greeted me like it was the first time I had been here. Moving to rub my face my right hand caught on something and wouldn't give. My attention quickly noticed that I was handcuffed to the railing of a hospital bed. Although tugging, pulling, and yanking wouldn't do any good I continued to try as the cuff clanged against the metal bed rail.

"Oh, good you're awake," said the dreaded voice of a man I recognized.

"Matteo! What is the *meaning* of this!" I tried to shout, pulling on the restraint of the handcuff.

"Careful you don't want to disturb it so much so that it closes down on your wrist more. That makes for a very uncomfortable time." He was smiling at me, mocking me – and still chewing on that *damn* toothpick.

"WHY AM I HANDCUFFED?" My vision blurred to red as I could kill him right now.

"Well before we answer that I think we need to start at the beginning – Claire why don't you fill your friend here in on what happened? She seems to be missing bits and pieces." I watched as Matteo stepped aside to let Claire through to my bedside.

"Claire? What's happening?" I asked breathlessly.

"Denver came in for his normal Thursday meal and he began asking all kinds of ridiculous questions about you like when you started going to *that* side of town and when you started using. I, of course, had no idea what he was talking about and practically called him crazy. You using? Never! That wouldn't even be a thought in your mind. Then he explained to me where he saw you and then he followed you to the restaurant and watched you go to your apartment. He said you could barely walk. You were swaying and holding onto anything you could get your hands on." She stopped to pull the chair closer to the bed before sitting down and taking my hand in hers.

"Is there more to this story Claire?" I asked in a harsh tone. Already irritated by the mention of Denver.

"He told me he was going up to check on you and he wanted me to stand at the bottom of the stairs in case we needed help. When he went inside, he found you on the floor – practically foaming at the mouth. He yelled down to me that you had overdosed and to call for an ambulance. On the way to the hospital, you began to come around and started talking about the craziest things like how you killed your husband and burned your house down with him still in it. The police didn't take that allegation lightly and they called Matteo to come and investigate."

"Thank you, Claire, that's enough," he said, putting his hand on her shoulder to stop her from continuing any further. I watched cautiously as he moved his hand to her back – giving her a few light pats. "I can handle it from here."

With that Claire got up and left the room, beginning to cry as she did.

"I can tell by the expression on your face that this is not how you pictured all this going down. Murder is a tough secret to keep locked inside. Even your subconscious was screaming to let it out." He seemed satisfied as he took a seat down on the chair and crossed his leg, brushing his pants off once he got comfortable.

"Oh, good you're awake!" a male doctor announced when he came in but neither Matteo nor I took our eyes off of each other.

"Well, what's the news Doc?" Matteo asked, impatient to learn about my condition.

After checking me over the doctor proclaimed I was fine. All of the drugs had been flushed out of my system and my body was responding normally. He told us that what I had overdosed on was rigged with something else. A mixture he had never seen before. He also said I was very lucky for my friend discovering my body and bringing me in so quickly. Any longer and I may not have survived.

"She's in perfect health, luckily. No damage that I can assess as of current. She's free to go," the doctor said, putting informative papers about substance abuse and where to get help on the table before leaving.

"Well, I don't know about *free* to go..." Matteo said under his breath after the doctor was out of the room. Shortly after, he too got up and walked out of the room and it was only then that I began messing with the handcuff once more.

A few seconds later two men accompanied Matteo back into the room.

"We've been looking for you a long time Miss Abriana," one of the officers said. "I have to hand it to you for almost getting away. Once your trail went cold, we had no idea where you might have gone. All hope seemed lost – that was until we got a tip-off from this area and met with Matteo to be filled in on the situation."

"You can't be serious," I said looking between the two of them and turning to Matteo. "Someone

157

drugged and almost killed me and instead of *investigating* that you're arresting me for a comment I made when I was under the influence of a drug! During a time when I had no idea what I was babbling on about? How does that even make sense?"

"Now, now – there's no talking your way out of this one Abriana. The secrets out and it's about high time you start playing nice. These two fine gentlemen have the pleasure of transporting you back to New Jersey where you'll be held before being tried and imprisoned." Matteo closed his arms across his chest in a satisfied manner. "You should've confessed to me, maybe we could've worked out some sort of deal," he said whispering in my ear. *Scum.* "Well, she's all yours boys! Here's the key to the cuffs." I watched as he handed over the tiny object before turning to me and winking as he left the room.

Fast Forward:

"Now how does it feel to cool your heels in jail?" I heard Matteo's voice ask from the other side of the bars. I never lifted my head to look at him. That was the last thing I wanted to do was give him, the satisfaction of seeing how much of a mess I really was.

"Sir please step aside," another man's voice instructed. "Abriana approach the bars."

I did what I was told, being sure to keep my head down the whole time.

"Alright you know the drill – turn around with your back flat against the cell door and put your hands up against the bars."

Once I was handcuffed to their satisfaction, they had me step away from the opening of the cell door. They held a tight grip on my arm as they guided me to the hearing.

"All rise!" the bailiff shouted after all the court members had entered the room. He then waited for everyone to stand before continuing. "The court is now in session; the honorable Judge Vailor is presiding."

Once Judge Vailor had taken his seat, the bailiff announced for everyone to sit. The time ticked by and all along I kept my head hanging low so that I would not have to make eye contact with anyone. I could hear the lawyer that was assigned to my case argue with the police officers that spoke. It sounded far off in the distance even though it was merely feet from me. Their arguments dragged on for what seemed like hours. My neck began to hurt from hanging it for so long.

After a closing statement was presented, a brief recess was held for the jury members to make their decision on whether or not I would be sent to prison for the crimes against me. During this time Judge Vailor had also disappeared through the same door he had come out of.

"How do you find the defendant?" These were the only words I heard before the ringing in my ears began.

"We the jury find the defendant..." I held my breath during the slight pause of the woman reading off the sentence of my life. "Not guilty, your honor."

"This is preposterous! It's an outrage!" Both officers yelled out.

"ORDER in my courtroom!" Judge Vailor yelled slamming down his wooden mallet.

Simultaneously everyone fell silent. It was all I could do but watch Judge Vailor flip through the pages of documents that lay in front of him. His eyes scanned the words of the pages quickly and without mercy. His brows were lowered and furrowed, he looked angry.

Before long, Judge Vailor removed his glasses to rub his eyes. "This is something I don't do often,

Miss Abriana," he said, attracting my attention. "But I am throwing this case out. Not only due to the lack of evidence but also due to the fact that all of which has been brought to me cannot be used in court. You are free to go."

And just like that, he slammed the mallet down, declaring this was over. The courtroom erupted in noise as Judge Vailor made his way through the door. It all seemed to happen so quickly. My handcuffs were removed and I was being ushered out of the courtroom.

All I remember as I left the building was Matteo's face. He was in complete disbelief of what had just happened. Removing his chewed toothpick, he slightly bent his body to bow at me, a congratulation for a job well done. But knowing all that I did about him, this was far from over.

I received a ride home from the police department as they felt the need to escort me there. Photographers and journalists alike wouldn't leave me alone in the slightest. Tonight, for the first time, I pushed a piece of furniture up against my apartment door after I locked it. Feeling even more unsafe that I had been thrown into the public eye. Would the family come for me now – knowing where I was? Had word already reached them, was

their arrival just around the corner? Did they follow
me home?

Chapter XVI

Unexpected

The days that followed were filled with the constant glance over my shoulder to see if I was being tailed. Several weeks had passed before I began to feel normal again. And with it came no surprise visits. Claire had moved on to bigger and better things – drooling over a new man once Denver stopped showing up. And for that I was thankful.

"Hey, can you lock up tonight?" Claire asked me one day as afternoon turned to evening. "My new hunk asked me to go on a date." Laughing at her puppy dog look – I agreed.

The rest of the evening flew by in a blur. Far into the after-hours of dinner, there hadn't been the usual number of guests – allowing me to do some detail cleaning before getting a head start on inventory counts.

Before long I was standing outside, pushing the key into the door and locking the place up for the night. The cooler air was crisp and the wind was sure to run a light rustling through my hair. Sending a chill to my neck and the newly revealed skin.

"Hey doll!" a voice I recognized said from behind me as I walked to my apartment door. "Fancy meeting you here again."

Before I could turn around to face the man I felt a blunt force to the head, knocking me off my feet. I rolled over onto my belly and grabbed my head with both hands. I could feel a warm liquid running into my palms. The sidewalk around me started to move and my eyes became crossed.

My body began to move without my consent, leading me to believe I was being dragged by someone. Everything around me was a blur. I could feel my body being lifted into a vehicle by two men. Even through my tainted vision, I could still make out the face of who was dragging my upper half into the backseat. It was Denver.

"Sorry about this Abriana, it's just business," he whispered to me before covering my face with a dark object.

I was so disoriented I couldn't even scream to let anyone around me know I was being kidnapped – that is if anyone was even around at this time of night. I had stayed at the restaurant later than normal to finish the rest of the inventory counts on our ingredients. This way I knew what I needed to send in for the order the next day. It was only until now that I regretted staying so long.

164

It seemed like hours I remained bound and blinded. The roads condition continued to get rougher to drive on as we bounced around in the car uncontrollably. "Can't you drive any faster? We got a schedule to keep," a man's voice whispered. Strangely it sounded like that of Matteo's.

"Yeah…yeah just shove another toothpick in that trap of yours why don't ya?" another man snapped. This time sounding eerily similar to Antonio.

"Will you two cut it out? You've been arguing ever since we left the city!" Denver said with a disgusted tone. "I've had it up to here."

After a long while, the car came to a harsh stop, propelling all of our bodies in a forward motion.

"Come on Abriana," I heard the man say that kept calling me doll. Pulling on my bicep he guided me out of the car, being sure to duck my head when it was appropriate.

Blinded, we walked on; I was completely dependent upon them to be my eyes. It was not a good feeling; they could be leading me to my death and I wouldn't know it. Although I had a strange suspicion that was exactly where we were heading.

My mind remained fuzzy, but fortunately for me, I was more aware of what was occurring than before. My hands were bound behind my back with handcuffs. I assumed they belonged to Matteo or Antonio. I couldn't see even a sliver of light through the material they had over my head. It held all the power.

Someone shoved me down onto the hard surface of what felt like a chair. Ripping the material from over my head I was blinded by the surrounding light. Squinting I saw nothing at first until my eyes adjusted to the brightness. The first thing I noticed was Denver off to the side holding a dark sack which I assumed was what was over my head the entire time.

Looking around the room I was in a run-down empty building. It held nothing but dirt, holes, and secrets. I could see the faces that I knew were already present – Matteo, Antonio, my attacker, and of course Denver. But there were other men present that I did not recognize. All five of them stood as straight as an arrow and were as silent as a graveyard.

They shot occasional glances my way but always gave me a look of disdain. I briefly wondered why all these men were brought here for little old me. Who were they? And who were they working for? Why was I here?

Immediately I began choking on the cloth they had tied around my mouth. It was twisted and soaked between my lips. I could feel the drool change from a steady drip to uncontrollably running out of the corner of my mouth. I was disgusted by it. I told myself I would scream bloody murder if they dared to remove it from me. Although the thought of doing that made me feel better, I also knew deep down that no one would ever hear my cries for help wherever we were. After all, that's why we had come to this place so that no one would hear me scream.

Judging by the looks of the additional men I would say they were all bad news. This only led me to believe what my subconscious told me all along – that Matteo and Antonio were crooked as well.

But how did they wind up with Denver? Where did he fit into all of this? And my attacker? How did they know him? Why was he even involved? Had the first time he put his hands on me been an inside job? How were they all connected to each other? But most importantly who went through all the trouble of bringing this group of people together?

Chapter XVII

Shadows

I hung my head to avoid any more unnecessary eye contact. None of them were talking and the room was as quiet as if it were empty of life entirely. Off in the distance, I could hear what sounded like faint footsteps. At first, I couldn't tell if they traveled away from us or if they were heading in our direction. But it didn't take me long to realize they were coming toward us.

Under my eyelashes, I could see that all of the men stood tall, straight, and unemotional. Even still no one was speaking. Occasionally I would see a head turn towards another but nothing more than that.

Eventually, the footsteps were so loud it was as if they were directly over top of me. And before long I felt whoever was hidden in the shadows had finally appeared. As the footsteps neared, they began to slow down in pace. With it I raised my head, watching as the men took turns nodding in the direction behind me. Still, everyone remained unspeaking.

"Cut her loose," a man's raspy voice commanded. The voice of my past. The voice I knew all too well. Ever so slowly pairs of goosebumps descended upon my body like polka dots. Randomly appearing and continuously sliding down my skin like raindrops.

After silently glancing around at each other, one of the men I didn't recognize decided to speak up. "You can't be serious boss. Do you have any idea what it took to get her here? Months and months of planning and watc–"

"I know. Now cut her loose," he repeated irritably.

Another one of the men I didn't know stepped forward while raising his pointer finger to the ceiling. "But boss–"

"I SAID CUT HER LOOSE DAMMIT! NOW!"

The booming voice of the angered man made me jump with fear. My body shook uncontrollably as his tone rang through my ears.

Matteo approached the chair I was bound to, keeping perfect eye contact. He looked angry, no doubt because of this whole situation. Kneeling down in front of me he cut the binding that held my ankles to the chair legs before moving behind me to release my bound wrists. Within seconds I could feel him untying the cloth that was knotted behind my head.

"Leave us," he said with rage, his tone being enough to make his point the first time.

As they departed, I rubbed my ankles lightly before standing and massaging my wrists.

"I've waited a long time for this moment," the man said as his footsteps continued to approach.

"I can *hardly* believe that." Already knowing who it was before I even turned around. "How are you alive Nicholas?"

"You mean you don't remember?" he asked in a whisper to my ear. His hands softly gripped my arms.

"Obviously I just need you to refresh my memory…" I whispered back.

"Here's what I recall…after you and I made eye contact – before you shot me – you quickly shut your eyes right before you pulled the trigger. And ever since I woke up from my coma I've been wondering why. Why did you close your eyes? Was it because you couldn't look at me when you did me dirty?"

"It was just business, Nicholas. Isn't that what you've said to me in the past? Every time you've broken me?"

"I don't know if we can compare what I did, to you shooting me." I could hear him slightly

170

chuckling behind me as he started rubbing my arms up and down.

"But I saw blood flooding the floor…" I said ignoring his comment.

"There's no denying you hit me in the head. You just didn't hit me where you thought you did. I have to say I expected your aim to be a little more on point than what it was."

"My aim was perfectly placed!" I said filled with anger as I jerked from his grip and finally turned to face him.

Upon making eye contact neither one of us said anything for a moment. Silently we both stood there looking at each other's faces. I could see his chest was heaving quickly. I could feel his breath in my face as he sucked in air at unnatural proportions. For this was the moment he had been waiting for. He had been hiding in the shadows patiently until he could come face to face with me once more.

Without losing our eye contact I could feel him touch my hand only to begin guiding it up to the middle of his face. His direction caught my attention as he did so. "Right here…close your eyes."

I could feel him lightly push my fingertips underneath the sunglasses he was wearing. He ran my hand over his left eyelid and then over his nose

171

before reaching his right eyelid. He let my fingertips rest upon it as he slowly opened it. Then to my horror, he pushed my fingers inside a hole that should not be there.

My eyes flung open and I began to scream as I tried to jerk back from his grip. But he squeezed my fingers together tightly, making it almost impossible to pull out of his grip. He continued to move my fingers, quickening the pace as he shoved them inside and outside of the wound so that I kept feeling the injury. He forced me to feel around the inside of the lid. Lining the opening of the empty eye socket I squirmed under his hold.

"Do you *see* what you did to me? You *took* something from me. But thankfully, it wasn't enough to kill me since it didn't reach my brain. The doctor said I was very lucky. I'll admit I never felt an impact like that before – it knocked me out cold – and on my ass, I might add. But between you and me I suppose I deserved it for all I did to you."

"You had it coming!" I almost spat as he finally released my hand.

"There's my girl. You still have that fire in you. I'm glad about that. Because I'm going to be the one to watch it die out. I'm going to smother that flame until there's nothing left of it." His voice made me tremble.

"But I *burned* the house down!" I blurted out – still in disbelief that he was standing before me, alive and well.

A snicker of a smile slowly began to form on his unharmed face, it almost sickened me. With those sunglasses on no one would even know he had an injury of any kind. I swear he could pull anything off. He twisted my stomach in a way I never thought I would feel again. "That you did my love, that you did. Thankfully Alberto was closer than the rest and was able to get me out of the back. He sustained some burns from the blaze but they were mild."

"Luckily, he was there…" I said disappointed. "Just think of what almost could've happened to you." *What should've happened to you.*

"If only you could grind your teeth anymore to say *luckily*. I can see you're not happy to see me but I am happy to see you." He wrapped his hand around my neck. Before this moment I had forgotten how large his hands were. Or rather how small my neck was – so much so that he could fit just one of his hands nearly around my entire neck. We stared each other down while he slowly walked me backward until a wall met my spine.

"So what? You're going to kill me now, huh? This is how it's going to end…just like this! Well, come on then! Get it over with already! Oh, Saint Nicholas finally gets his revenge." I mockingly laughed in his face, hoping that with any luck this would poke him enough to end it all quickly.

I had never imagined how Nicholas would kill me. I never thought our relationship would ever reach this point. But if I had to picture it, I would've thought by gun and not by strangling. Maybe now he realized he would receive greater pleasure in watching the light leave my eyes than a hole in my heart.

He removed his sunglasses so that I could stare into the empty eye socket. The taste of vomit worked its way to the back of my throat as I was repulsed by the sight of it. Looking at it too long I noticed a small bit of dried pus clung to his lower eyelashes, making my insides turn. It was revolting. "Love, this isn't how this works. I know you feel…powerful because you shot me but you're in *my* world now. It's *my* rules. And regretfully the words coming from your mouth *won't* make me kill you any faster. You're going to *suffer* slowly and painfully but first I want to see it happen mentally before physically."

He ran his thumb over my mouth, smiling like the devil in my face as he showed his sharpened teeth. I could feel my pupils widen at his remark,

174

knowing by the motion what would come next. I began to recall the memory from years ago seeing one of his Russian friends do this same gesture to a young girl. Later he explained to me what it meant. I shuddered under his grasp at the recollection, attempting to jerk my face away from him.

I couldn't believe that this was the man I once adored, even loved. How could I have been so blind? I cursed myself for everything we were. I just wanted it all to be over and if death was the only way – then so be it. I had played my card and now it was his turn to play his. But I always knew if by some chance he hadn't died, I couldn't even prepare myself enough for when he found me. And he would find me. And when he did…he would kill me.

Chapter XVIII

Stolen

"I can see my new appearance is making you quite uncomfortable…allow me to make myself better suited for your liking." He turned his back on me briefly before looking back at me, this time with two eyes.

I reached for his face. "But how–"

"You should know my connections by now Abriana." He knocked my hand down before I could touch him.

"It's fake. A glass eye. Quite a likeness is it not?" He pointed to his real one so that I could look between the two to notice any differences. "I was in a coma for a long time…so they told me," Nicholas began to explain as he walked me out of the room, we were standing in. "Like I said the doctor told me I was very lucky the bullet didn't travel inside any farther because if it would've hit my brain I most likely wouldn't have survived. Actually, his exact words were that I would have been dead before I hit the ground."

"Then why the most likely?" I asked confused if it were so matter-of-factly.

"Because he said no matter how many times you try to get rid of me, I always find a way to just keep coming back. He told me it *must* be love."

"And he *must* be delusional."

To this, he erupted with laughter.

"Miss Abriana," a warm voice said pulling my attention from Nicholas. It was Alberto. Unknowingly we had traveled outside to a parked car. Alberto stood patiently with the door open.

I rested my hand softly on his chest. "I'm sorry," I whispered to him, getting a look at the scars on the side of his face along with the burn mark on his hand.

"I'll always forgive you, dear," he said lovingly.

"You are too kind to her, too generous. She'd kill you if she had the chance or if she needed to." I watched that snake of a smile spread across Nicholas's face once more. He was satisfied with his interruption.

"He knows me better than that," I said looking back at Alberto.

"She would never kill me, Nicholas...because if it ever came down to it, I would kill her first."

As much as I wanted to let my mouth fall open to his remark, I kept calm and tried to appear unbothered by his comment. *He swore he'd always protect me. Maybe things change when you try to kill their boss and then burn them in the process.*

Climbing into the car, the first fifteen minutes or so of our ride were dead silent until I finally built up the courage to ask, "So you were the one who paid to get me out – the bail I mean?"

Without hesitation, he admitted to it. "I wanted to make you squeal but not allow the system to punish you too much. I wanted to do that part."

"I assume then that the break-in was you too?"

"What break-in?" he asked, snapping his head in my direction.

Throwing my hands up in the air I began to shout, already irritated with his games. "You expect me to believe you?"

"No, I don't but I am telling you the truth!" he shouted back.

"Oh, come now! I know you came inside our house! Don't play dumb Nicholas–"

I hadn't even finished my sentence before he struck me across the face. The slap stung for a minute and I remained quiet as I stared outside the window that was away from him. I held my cold hand over top of the slapped cheek to try to cool the sting.

"I'm *warning* you, to watch your *mouth* Abriana. Don't speak to me like that."

"What are you going to do? Huh? Kill me?" I taunted him.

I barely let out a gasp as his closed fist punched me in the face rendering me unconscious.

Fast Forward:

The next thing I remember is waking up in an unfamiliar bedroom. My nose hurt and my head pounded. Everything around me was still and silent. Making my way to the door I found it to be unlocked – which was something I wasn't expecting. The hallway was long and my head spun as I hugged the wall while walking.

I could hear the sound of clanging coming from somewhere below. I recognized it as silverware banging off of dishware. The closer I got to the room the more pieces of conversation I could hear. The smell of food made my mouth water and I suddenly felt as if I would die of starvation if I couldn't eat.

Stumbling into a formal dining room I saw Denver, Nicholas, Matteo, and Antonio all comfortably seated and enjoying a warm meal. Their gabs became hushed when I entered the room.

"You're awake!" Denver announced jumping out of his seat to greet me like an old friend. "Here

– sit here." He pulled out a chair for me next to Nicholas.

"Everyone out," Nicholas said in a demanding manner.

Denver paused by his side while he grabbed his plate, "Do you want me to bring Abriana in a dish? Or would you like me to have Nario send something in for her?"

The name Nario circled in my mind. My sweet Nario, the kind of joyous pleasure I enjoyed having around. At that moment I missed his jokes and his laugh. But mostly I missed his cooking. His talent would never go unremembered for as long as I live. I could almost taste his old dishes on the tip of my tongue. I silently thanked the heavens that he too had lived, since he was another who was nothing but good to me. Before I could request to see him, Nicholas's voice disrupted my thoughts.

"No, I'll get it." His voice was stone cold. Once everyone had left, he commanded me to sit before getting up and leaving the room.

I was confused as this was not the sort of punishment, I was expecting to be enduring from him.

"Eat," Nicholas said as he shoved a small bowl of soup at me. "You look like you haven't in days."

"That sounds about right," I said without looking up.

Hearing the chair pull out beside me, he regained his position next to me. I watched out of the corner of my eye as he took his seat.

"Where are we?" I barely waited for him to be completely sitting down before I asked the question.

"Hidden away from the world." I could hear the hint of a smile wanting so desperately to spread across his lips.

"I gathered that but where are we precisely?"

"Our exact location," he began in an exasperated tone. "We are a long way from my family for the time being. That's all you need to know."

Blowing on my first spoonful of soup I couldn't help but swallow hard when he mentioned his family. "Do they know I'm with you?"

"No, don't worry you're safe from them...for now." He let out a small chuckle hidden under his breath. "I'm sure they'd like some time to punish you too...in their own way."

"If they would've had it their way, I'd be dead by now, I'm sure."

"They don't know it was you that did all of this." I could hear the seriousness in his voice and knew that he wasn't lying this time.

"They don't…" I repeated in astonishment. Partly because they hadn't found out yet and partly because he hadn't personally told them.

Lightly I could hear the tapping of fingertips on the table, which were not mine. "We have many things to discuss."

"Such as?" I asked without giving him the satisfaction of being able to look at my face.

"For starters let's talk about *Benson*."

Chapter XIX

Gambler

I'm afraid I didn't understand at all what he meant by that and I hadn't the slightest idea of where this conversation was going to go.

"What about Benson?" I lifted my head to meet him eye to eye.

"Do you know what kind of business he was involved in?" he asked almost sympathetically.

"Involved in?" I repeated, rolling my eyes. "I think there's been some kind of a mistake."

"He was mixed up in some bad business Abriana. You have to know that's why he was murdered." I looked down to catch his hand balling up into a fist.

"I'm afraid I didn't know that at all. Are you sure we are talking about the same person? The little old man who ran a run-down bookstore? He basically had the word fragile written on his forehead. And temperamentally sarcastic on his back."

"That's the one," he said finally breaking our eye contact. "Didn't you ever wonder where he got the money to fix up that bookstore?"

"No…he and Denise had money. They had been saving all their lives, they–"

"Lies, lies, LIES! He fed them to you and you ate them up like Thanksgiving dinner. They didn't have money. In fact, they barely had a penny to their name. They were making ends meet by the skin of their teeth. Denise couldn't get the proper care she needed because of the irresponsibleness of her own husband."

"I don't believe you!" I shouted, throwing my spoon across the table at the wall. "You don't know a thing about him! He would never jeopardize her health, he loved her!"

"Fine. Then don't, why would you? I wouldn't have expected you to. In fact, it would've been preposterous if you had." Aside from throwing his arms in the air nonchalantly. His reaction was calm. Calmer than it should've been and that alone frightened me.

"He had an addiction." His fists came slamming down on the table making everything on it jump. "He was a heavy gambler Abriana, he couldn't help it! You may *think* you knew him but you had no idea what he was really like, who he really was. He was fighting battles of his own!"

"Stop it!" I shouted as I stood and covered my ears with my hands. When he stood before me, I began taking small steps back.

"He also couldn't help cheating the wrong people and stealing them out of their money. He was hungry for it! He was starving for green like a wolf wanting meat! And even if by chance he was doing it to pay for Denise to get some help that doesn't make it right! In their eyes that doesn't excuse it!" With every step I took back he walked forward, attempting to keep the same distance between us.

"You're LYING!" I said bumping into the corner of the table while I was rounding it.

"Why do you think their kids never came around huh? Think about it. He sobered up after some time. Maybe even becoming a better man. So why didn't they ever *come* home? Did you ever stop and ask yourself that? I bet Denise never mentioned that while you were taking care of her. During those days when you were nursing her back to health!"

"How do you know that? And how do you know what I was doing with Denise?"

"BECAUSE I KNOW EVERYTHING YOU DID! I KNOW EVERY MOVE YOU EVER MADE. Because I have eyes everywhere!" He continued marching towards me with harder footsteps this time. "He almost had them fooled until he didn't. It took them a while before they caught onto their missing money but they did. They always do. And that's one thing you don't ever mess with is a mafia's money."

"Who's they?" I demanded, even though I already knew he'd never say.

My spine met something hard and unmoving as I soon realized he had backed us into a wall. I watched as his fist came up to his cheekbone before he thrust it forward. I squeezed my eyes shut and turned my face away from the impact. I could hear the cracking as his fist met the wall, punching it hard next to my head.

We stood there silently. Listening to each other's breathing. I kept my eyes shut until I heard the removal of his fist from the wall and with it, the sound of his breathing returned to normal.

"How did he cheat?" I asked in a whisper, keeping my eyes closed and my face still turned away from him.

"He hid the cards he wanted to keep. Normally cheaters will hide their cards up their sleeves or under the table. Whatever way he did it helped him to make big gains when he played poker against them. Benson was a smart man; I just can't believe he never thought they would catch on eventually. The years he had been around…he knew better."

I wiped my eyes with the back of my hand before sniffing at my runny nose.

"I'm sorry about Benson," he finally said as I opened my eyes to look at him. "I know how much he meant to you."

"He did…" I began to tear up recalling my rambunctious old man. "He meant a lot to me, more than I could ever explain to you."

"I know…" he said as he held our eye contact and stepped away from me. He returned to the table once more and took his seat without looking back at me.

My stomach had begun to growl again, reminding me I hadn't yet finished my dinner. I kept my eyes fixed on Nicholas as he ran his hands feverishly through his hair.

"I'll get you another spoon," he said, jumping up as I sat down.

"Did you know the Greco's too?" I asked when he returned with the silverware.

"Know them personally…no. But I had them investigated to the best of my ability even before we had gotten married."

My eyes flicked up to his.

"Well…before you married Gabriele I should say."

"That's more like it," I said with a smile. "Because I know for sure if you would've ever asked me to marry you, I would've said no."

"I had a strange hunch. That's why I had to turn into someone else entirely," he laughed at both himself and me. I laughed too in a disturbing kind of way.

"What did you know about them?" I asked, picking up our old conversation. "Did you know about Nannina then…since you know everything?"

"You know there are times I wish you weren't such a smart mouth and other times I think I would miss it if it wasn't that way." He smiled in his devilish way to let me know his thoughts were disturbed.

"I hate you," I whispered through clenched teeth.

"I know you do baby…but that hate you feel now doesn't compare to the hate you'll feel later. I can promise you that." Sending a wink my way his devilish smile had turned into a grin.

I glared at him in silence, not wanting to know the meaning behind his words.

In a huff, he confessed he knew about Nannina as he excused himself from the table and began to pace the floor. Eventually, he wandered over to the buffet and pulled out a container of hard alcohol.

I watched him throw back shots in silence, one after the other like it was nothing. He made no face and sounded no noise. His movements were quick and had been perfected over time. The steady hand poured. The head snapped back. And the cycle continued in an endless fashion.

It seemed as if he had downed a fifth before he stopped himself and hid the bottle away once more. Tapping his mouth lightly with a handkerchief he returned to almost a gentlemanly state.

"Now...where were we?" he asked, cocking his head to one side.

"Nannina."

Chapter XX

Secrets

"I am shocked the Greco's didn't tell you or maybe they didn't want to alarm you…"

"Tell me what…exactly?" Nicholas was full of secrets and I never understood how he knew so many of them. Better yet how he seemed to be involved in so many of them.

"Nannina was strangled in her sleep. Dirty cops told Giorgia and her husband it was suicide. But I know better than that."

I could feel myself slipping off the chair. "What? You can't strangle yourself in bed…"

"Bingo! That's my girl! You most certainly cannot. So, what do they do? They come up with an elaborate story that she tried to hang herself beforehand. Being completely unsuccessful BUT damaging her windpipes enough that she crawled into bed exhausted from her attempt. Leading her to pass away once she fell asleep."

"Tell me they didn't believe that! It's preposterous!" Jumping out of my seat, my chair came crashing to the floor with a thud. "It was foul play, Nicholas!"

"I know it was my dear," he said taking a seat at the head of the table, far away from me.

"Did they question it?" I asked wildly.

"That I don't know. I would certainly hope so but I can't say for sure."

"Why in the world would someone kill Nannina? She was the sweetest, kindest old lady you ever met!"

"Are you asking my opinion?" When I said nothing, he continued with his theory. "She had something that someone knew about and they came to break in and steal it. She was supposed to be at work and oh what a surprise it was when Nannina arrives home early on the day the robbery is in progress–"

"Wait! How do you know all this?" Rubbing my forehead with confusion all I could do was stare at him in disbelief. *Had he been in on it? How does he know all these details? It's like he was there.*

"Isn't it obvious? I was there of course!"

In less than a second, I was charging at him. "I'LL KILL Y–"

Pushing himself up from the table he grabbed my hands just as I got to him, stopping me in my tracks. "Okay…in hindsight that *may* have been a *bad* joke."

"WHAT? I *swear* to God…" I fought against his restraints as hard as I could.

"What? What are you going to do baby? Kill me? You tried that once and didn't succeed. I don't think next time you'll be successful either. In fact, your biggest mistake was not killing me when you have the chance. But soon though…you'll wish you had." He held both of my wrists in one of his hands so he could push the hair from my face in a loving manner. *Sicko.*

Spitting at him went nowhere. It simply ran down my chin and dripped off as I forgot how to propel it out of my mouth.

"An adorable slob you are…" he mocked before shoving me away from him and taking his seat once more. "Sit."

I kept silent as I followed his command, returning to my overturned chair.

"Matteo was called to investigate. He and Antonio both." He rubbed his hands together so hard I swore the friction would catch them on fire.

"And you had *nothing* to do with it, of course," I mocked back.

"Of course. What kind of monster do you take me for? I wouldn't kill an old lady in cold blood. What would I want from her? I have everything I need. Well...*now* I have everything I need." He motioned to me during his final words.

"Did they find out anything? Or were they just as useless as they always were?" I said with disdain.

"They found nothing that I know of. The trail has been cold ever since. Whoever did this, knew what they were doing and it was none of our people." He shook his head from side to side a few times before stopping to rub his temples. "I'm sorry my dear, you know how I hate to be the bearer of bad news to you..."

I continued glaring at him from my seat. "Yet you always seem to be. The bad news follows you like a foul smell." He smiled wickedly at me, the one I both adored and hated. "Were there any rumors of the object she had...circulating?"

He pondered for a moment, rubbing the tabletop with his fingers as he did. "I remember...a long time ago when her husband passed away that he had left her something very valuable. A family heirloom of sorts. It had always been locked away because it was worth so much value. People would kill for it. The story goes that their ancestors were archaeologists and something had been found during an excavation. There was a struggle between the two partners and one of them was killed. The other fled with the possession and hid it away for years, only to be seen during its turnover to the next generation. No one ever spoke of the object itself. It was kept very quiet at all times."

"Well, if that's true then how did they know Nannina had it and where it even was?" I said with frustration.

"All good questions. What I'm about to say is all hear-say so keep that in mind…apparently, the partner who was killed, his son was also present during the dig and he witnessed from afar the struggle. It was his family's mission to search for what they believed is there's. Never stopping until it is been returned to its rightful owners."

"Do the cops know who this rival family is? Have they questioned them?" I asked breathlessly.

"No dear, I don't think they know. Nor do they care – as I said they are dirty cops."

"But if that's the case then what's in it for them – not to pursue it?" I asked confused by his answer.

"There are times when certain actions happen that they just don't care about. They don't want to overexert time and money into a case that has already gone cold, especially with nothing to go on."

"So, what…" I said with a huff. "They will just close the case and be done with it?"

"No…I'd imagine they'd leave it open – let it linger that way for some time to appease the family and then after many years close it. This just isn't something they'll continue to look into."

"But why not Nicholas? Can't you *make* them?"

With this, he burst into laughter. The deep laugh pulled from his chest. "What are you saying? Make them? They're cops Abriana."

"Don't laugh me off! Your family runs the dirty cops – they practically work for your family and always have! I hate when you treat me like I don't know what I'm talking about like I'm stupid!"

"Oh no, you're certainly not that Abriana. I learned that lesson the hard way when you shot a bullet into my head, remember that?" His mocking only infuriated me further.

"I *hate* you!" Blurting it out of nowhere I hesitated briefly once those words had come out of my mouth.

"No, you don't," he said chuckling a few times. "You may even think that you do but you don't. You wish you could though, more than anything you wish you could."

He had *no* idea how I felt. He thought he knew but he truly didn't.

After the silence was extended between us, he said, "I'll have someone look into the case. I can't promise that it'll go any further than it already has."

"That's better than nothing," I said in a much softer voice than I had been using with him.

He merely chuckled once, so lightly I almost didn't catch it. "Regardless of everything that happened between us…I do love you Abriana," he said clearing his throat, almost seeming to be a little choked up on his own words. "I'd do anything for you. There is no limit, there's nothing that I wouldn't do for you if you really wanted."

"Why are you telling me this Nicholas?"

"I know it doesn't change anything but I just want you to know how deeply I still feel for you and how much you mean to me."

I didn't know what he expected of me. His eyes were glazed over and he stared at me intently. I said nothing before looking away from him and down at the table. After everything we had gone through – the past and the present. I couldn't bring myself to love him anymore. I couldn't tell him what wasn't true. I would never love him again. I had nothing left to give to him. He had drained my body and soul and it was something I could never recover from.

Chapter XXI

Untote

Nicholas slowly stood, brushing off his outfit as he did and straightening his upper half. "I have something to show you...this will either be the breaking point or perhaps even a reconciliation – it all depends on how you look at it."

I swallowed hard on the frightening calmness that came over him. "I don't like the sound of that..."

"Please follow me," he said as he gestured for me to take his hand while I stood from the table.

"Where are we going?" I asked as we approached the staircase in the center of the foyer.

"The thing I have to show you is upstairs," he said almost in a whisper.

Hesitantly, I quietly followed him up the winding staircase to not the first floor but the second. A balcony overlooked the floors below and the hallway went on endlessly with more and more doors. I could see a light coming from underneath the very last one at the end of the hall.

The closer we got the louder the sounds from within became. Nicholas grabbed the doorknob and took a long hard look at my face. "Are you ready to see what is behind this door?"

I attempted to swallow the knot in my throat but it didn't move. "Yes..."

"Try not to scream, my dear."

The door opened to a room colored in pink paint. Shelves hung on the walls with dolls in fancy dresses. Toys were scattered on the right side of the room, one of which was a child-size wooden rocking horse. A bed fit for a princess was on the left side of the room. A canopy was beautifully hung above the top of the bed.

I could hear soft mumbling followed by clanging coming from the side of the bed that I couldn't see. Following the noise, I saw a large dollhouse with a little girl seated with her back to me. She was playing with one of her dolls. I watched her silently as she walked the toy up the staircase, talking to it in words that I didn't understand.

Nicholas wrapped his hands around my shoulders gently before whispering into my ear. "This is Gesella. Gesella Jemma Manchini."

"You have a daughter?" I whispered back.

His lips hovered close to my earlobe. "Does that come as a surprise to you my dear?"

"It does…" I turned quietly to face him so that we wouldn't startle the child. "And where is the Mrs. at?"

"It's funny that you say that actually…" he said blushing.

I simply cocked my head unsure of what to make of his reaction. "Where…is she?" I repeated once more.

"There is no Mrs. and there never was." He said scratching the back of his neck nervously.

Motioning behind me I stared at him curiously. "Then who is the mother of this child? You can't make a human on your own–"

"You are my love."

Stammering back in disbelief a wave of shock came over me. "I'm afraid I don't understand what you're saying at all."

"Gesella is your child, your daughter. The one you had with…Danny."

Grabbing his arm, I pulled him over to the far corner of the room where I could speak to him louder. "But that's impossible! How dare you, Nicholas! Of all the cruel things you've ever done or said to me! You know I lost my child during my fall!"

"Sadly, it was all a lie, my dear. Your nurse was paid off not to say anything about the baby being born. She lied to you because she was instructed to. Your baby was alive and did live and you had it naturally."

"NICHOLAS! I think I'd remember if I birthed a child!"

"I know this is all a bit of a shock to you," he said softly.

"A bit!" I almost shouted.

"Sit down a moment please, let me explain." He gestured to a table and chairs set up near us. "Have you ever heard of *Twilight Sleep?*"

"No...should I have? What did you do Nicholas? What did you do!" I started to cry as he began to tell me what happened.

"There was a doctor from Germany visiting the hospital at the time you had been brought in. The clinic he worked at specialized in many practices and this *twilight sleep* happened to be one of them. How it was explained to me was the patient is given a generous combination of morphine and scopolamine. These two together calm the nervous system and help it to be free of pain and allows you to fall into a virtually unconscious state. That's why you have no memory of it. From what I was told when you're under this type of sedation there is normally no recollection of a woman giving birth to a child along with any associated pain that would've come from it."

"But how did the baby physically come out of me? Normally women have to push Nicholas!" I said in outrage at everything he had just explained to me.

"She was forcibly removed from you…with forceps. That's how it's done over there and it has always been a success."

"A success…you call *this* a success? You sick bastard!"

"Yes, call me insane, but I do consider this a success! She would've died if they didn't get her out of you! You should be thankful!"

"I hate you! Oh, how I hate you!"

"You feel that way now but you won't when you spend time with her. All that hate and anger you feel in this moment will melt away."

"And how *dare* you give her *your* last name! She's not *your* child!"

"She was mine because I had to raise her! I've been raising her! I have just as many fatherly rights to her as Danny! I have been the father figure in her life!"

"How dare you say that! And what a father figure you are, only by choice did you raise her! If I would've known she was alive that never would've happened!"

"We could go back and forth about this but it's honestly exhausting. The doctor saved not only your life but hers as well. He stayed with you for several hours to regulate your dosage and keep a close eye on you. He was very impressed with how well you did. He said normally women need to wear dark glasses and earplugs to avoid overstimulation but in your case, it wasn't necessary."

"Did he say why they usually put those on women?"

"There have been many cases of women thrashing around. When that happens, they have hit their heads or clawed at themselves. Relentless screaming is almost always present and they have to be restrained to the bed by any means necessary."

"Any means necessary. What does that even mean?" I asked appalled.

"Restrained by wrists or ankles. Sometimes even by straight jackets."

"That's horrible Nicholas!" I said with disgust.

"It's only for the health and safety of the patient Abriana."

"He told me a story that went horribly wrong – where he had to blindfold the woman with a towel around her head. She was then placed in a cot bed so that she didn't fall on the floor. And he had to bind her to get her to stop rolling around. If that wasn't bad enough, she screamed for hours and had to lay in her vomit and waste until she had given birth. It was nineteen hours of labor."

"And after all that was the baby okay when it was born?" I asked holding my breath.

"Her baby was born drugged up because of the mixture. It happens with every child done this way. It was unable to breathe normally at first so he had to resort to slapping it upside down on the back. They use this often to revive comatose newborns."

"So, is this what happened to Gesella? Was my child drugged up in a comatose state? WAS SHE? Did he *hit* my child?"

"Momma," a soft voice said to me as I felt a light pull on the bottom of my shirt.

Chapter XXII

Inseparable

Looking down, my eyes fell upon the most beautiful brown-haired green-eyed baby I had ever seen. She was smiling at me and holding her arms in the air for me to pick her up.

Without hesitation, I scooped her up in my arms and rubbed her back lightly. We stared at each other in silence before she began to play with my necklace – the chain hanging dangerously close to my throat.

"Careful. She'll strangle you with that," he joked in his serious manner.

I smiled without looking in his direction.

"I'll leave you two alone to spend some time together. Bring her down for dinner, it'll be ready in a few hours."

I ran my hand over her head. Allowing her hair to run across my hand so that I could feel the softness of it. I kissed her forehead lightly and began to bounce her on my hip while walking around the room holding her in my arms. I didn't know what came over me. It was as if my motherly side kicked in and suddenly, I knew all too well what to do.

She smelled so good. It was the smell of a child – one that can't be described. She smiled up at me from time to time, even laughing sweetly as we moved around the room together.

She laid her head on my chest and let out what sounded like a sigh of relief. I too laid my head on hers and began to hum her a sweet melody. Within a minute she began to squirm in my arms signifying that she wanted to be put down.

Once her feet touched the floor, she took off running towards the wooden rocking horse, pausing briefly to look at me before trying her best to climb on top of it. I rushed to her side to help her so that she didn't hurt herself trying. But when she had difficulty rocking it on her own, she silently looked to me for help. And without any words between us, I knew she wanted me to rock her.

That lasted only a minute or two before she was struggling to climb down from it. Scrambling to help her once more she took off again, this time back towards her dollhouse. She stopped when she reached it before turning to look at me, this time to see if I had followed her which I had not. I was still standing – quite dumbfounded by this entire situation – near the rocking horse.

"Momma!" she shrieked excitedly as she burst into laughter. I watched quietly while she ran back in my direction. Grabbing my hand, she tried her best to pull me and take me back to the dollhouse. Together we sat for a long while and played doll.

More time had passed than we both knew and as the sun began to set for the evening, I noticed that Gesella grew fussy. It started with her throwing her dolls in irritation. Then it switched to her falling to the floor and rolling around. And after a few minutes of that then the tears came on suddenly – her silence rolling into screams of discomfort.

Nicholas came barging into the room – scaring us both half to death. "I didn't do anything!" I said in a panic, throwing my arms up in the air as if I was getting arrested.

"I know you didn't dear, it's alright. When she gets like this, she's either hungry or tired and it's our job to figure out which one," he said calmly. His soft tone soothed her enough so he could scoop her up in his arms. She squirmed around a little longer before finally quieting down and beginning to suck her thumb. "I'm guessing by the time of day she's probably ready for dinner and I am assuming you are too."

I watched as he pulled her thumb from her mouth and told her not to do that. Afterward, he caressed her head softly while she rested it on his shoulder. I followed behind him in silence while she watched me over his broad form. The both of us kept our eyes locked on each other.

When we were almost to the staircase she reached for me – extending one of her little arms out as far as she could while the other remained around his neck. He whispered soft coos into her ear to keep her from throwing another tantrum which seemed to be working. I quickened my pace to hold her little hand with mine before we started the descent when I would be unable to hold on.

Her tiny fingers were squeezing mine to keep me from being able to detach from her mighty grip. I smiled at her, making funny faces occasionally to keep her cheerful. She giggled at me along the way – her smile reaching her eyes, making them twinkle with pure happiness.

Gesella warmed my heart and gave me a reason to live again. And Nicholas had been right – spending time with her melted all my anger and worries away. She made me feel whole again – she had taken my emptiness and filled it with love and innocence.

My biggest regret was not being by her side since the day she was born. But from this time forward I vowed to never allow anything or anyone to separate us ever again. She meant too much to me and I feared my whole world would be torn apart if we couldn't be together.

Reaching the staircase, we headed towards the familiar dining room. A height chair fit for a princess was already seated at the table. This was an object that had not occupied the space before. "Okay Gesella, is my baby ready to eat?" Nicholas asked her in a lovingly fatherlike tone.

Although he meant no harm in saying it, I couldn't help but feel a certain twinge of irritation and jealousy towards him. Stepping into her life, taking over as the father figure, getting to spend time with her and enjoy her company, and getting to love her longer than I.

"How did you manage to raise her while you were chasing after me all those years?" I asked him blatantly as he was fastening her height chair belt across her belly.

"Whatever do you mean, my dear?" he asked me sweetly.

Rolling my eyes behind him, I crossed my arms harshly across my chest, continuing to watch her touch his face and hair – giggling nonstop while she did. "My apologies, I didn't realize the question wasn't as clear as it could have been. What I am meaning to ask is where was Gesella while you were with me? Both in Atlantic City and in New

Jersey? Who was raising her while you spent every waking day with me?"

"My mother," he said matter-of-factly. "And of course, Raphael was there. He stayed behind to protect her and watch over the rest of the family. But his main duties were to keep a close eye on her. Once I decided what the right thing to do was, I had Raphael take her to my family's estate in Chicago. I figured that would be the safest place for her for the time being."

When he stood to face me, I slapped him as hard as I could across the face. So hard in fact that the palm of my hand stung – leaving behind an invisible red hand print on the side of his cheek. "You son of a bitch!"

Just then Gesella began screaming and crying. She reached in both of our directions but neither one of us moved from our stare down with the other.

Chapter XXIII

Prayers

"Hey, hey, hey – what's going on in here?" Nario announced rushing to her side. "It's okay sweetie! Mommy and Daddy are just having a grownup talk, that's all." He lightly rubbed her back in circles.

She began to calm down though her face remained flushed and her eyes puffy from the tears. Before long she was reaching for him to pick her up.

"There, there! Now, what do you say you and I go into the kitchen and get a pre-dinner snack, huh?" he asked her, unbuckling the belt. "What do you think Dad, does that sound like a good idea?" Without looking up at Nicholas he waited for a response from him while picking her up.

His eyes remained dark and fixed on me entirely. His mouth was in a firm scowl, though between clenched teeth he managed to speak. "I think that would be best…thank you Nario."

Once the two of them were out of the room Nicholas began to lightly rub his cheek. "You got a good hit on me that time little girl." I could hear the anger in his tone though he tried his best to control it.

"You *took my* child to *your* family's home and let them raise her. And if that wasn't enough, you left her under Raphael's watch and care! You know I *hated* him! I never trusted that man! And I never trusted *you!* I should've made sure you were dead."

"You're right – you should have. But you didn't and that's why we are where we are right now." He smirked devilishly in my direction.

"You make me *sick* Nicholas!"

"I know my dear, I know."

"Everything okay in here? I heard there was quite a scuffle happening?" Raphael asked, stepping into view as he walked leisurely into the dining room.

"Everything is fine Raphael – you can return to the kitchen so that Abriana and I can finish our conversation before dinner."

Motioning like a soldier saluting to his captain, he retrieved – excusing himself from the room.

"What would you have had me do instead? I'm open to hearing any bright ideas that may have formed inside that interesting head of yours."

Mocking me would get him nowhere. It only infuriated me further. In my head flashed a thousand different ways to kill him, being victorious this time around.

"Her mother would have been the one to raise her – that was the only solution. I should have you locked up for kidnapping!"

"Oh, please do!" I watched as he held his hands up to pray. "Won't that be an interesting turn of events since the cops are on my family's payroll?"

He was having fun with this. He saw absolutely nothing wrong with what he had done and therefore would take no responsibility or accountability for his actions. In his twisted mind, he raised another man's daughter whom he had shared with the love of his life. He should be seen as a saint in my eyes. A saint he would never be.

"I'm leaving here with my daughter right after dinner," I said with disgust.

"We'll discuss your options," he said with a serious tone, throwing in a wink at the end.

"My opt–"

"Dinners served!" Nario declared, joyfully clapping his hands together.

Neither of us had noticed that while we went back and forth arguing, Nario had been fast at work filling the table with food.

"Come now you two!" he said putting his hands on his hips. "We have a lot to be thankful for today. Our *family* is back together and we have this little one to enjoy in our lives now. There's so much we need to be grateful for and we just need to celebrate and enjoy this time together!" Unfortunately, Nario was right and if anyone could bring us together for a good meal – it would be him.

Raphael along with the rest of the men entered the room for dinner. He carried Gesella in his arms and she was loving every minute of yanking on his gray hair and laughing at his pain.

"You have a Manchini on your hands here Nicholas. There's no doubt about that!"

Nicholas began to chuckle before abruptly stopping to look at my expression. But I however was staring down Raphael – hoping to melt the skin off his bones with my glare. Once he got her buckled into her height chair he took the seat next to her, smiling up at me as he did. I thought of diving over the table at him – lunging at him with all my might. But I wouldn't get to him before one of the men would grab me, that was for certain.

"Would you like to sit next to Gesella?" Nicholas whispered to me.

"No, I would not," I said as loud as I could. "I wish to sit next to Raphael."

"Ooo–goody for me!" he said mockingly while laughing with the guys.

"What are you *doing?*" Nicholas asked in a rather harsh tone while I was attempting to stroll

213

past him. When I didn't respond right away, he grabbed my arm and yanked me back in his direction.

"Nothing at all…*dear*, just trying to take my seat for dinner. That's all." I gave him too much of a sweet smile. Just like that, I think he knew I had something evil formulating inside of me.

Before dinner started, we bowed our heads to pray like we always had – Nario led the prayer this time which was something I wasn't used to. "Bless us Oh Lord, and these thy gifts, which we are about to receive, from thy bounty, through Christ, Our Lord. Amen."

It came as no surprise to me that Nicholas was the first to see what had happened while everyone's heads hung down to pray. His reaction was perfect. "What…have you done…Abriana?" He breathed slowly in and out. His face didn't appear angry nor did his eyes. His hands were simply levitating off the table as if he was surrendering to an arrest. "Easy now. Everyone listens to exactly what I say. Nobody moves and everyone remain calm."

Ever so slowly I smiled as I pulled the steak knife from Raphael's neck. The one I had shoved deep inside one of his carotid arteries. Once the knife had been pulled from his neck, blood began to squirt out – continuing to drain from his body. He was dead within minutes because of how quickly those main arteries can bleed out. Everyone watched in silence as his body slumped onto the table – flattening his plate of food.

"She killed him! SHE KILLED HIM!" Nario screamed out.

It was during the same time that Gesella began to cry and scream out of pure fright at the yelling voices that emerged.

"I said everyone REMAIN CALM!" Nicholas screamed at the top of his lungs while pounding on the table – silencing everyone. Afterward, he stood silently, taking a moment to brush off his shirt. He instructed the rest of the men to get Raphael out of the dining room and clean up the mess. He then turned to Nario and told him to take Gesella into the kitchen and feed her so that she could be put down for a nap.

Chapter XXIV

Disappearance

After Raphael's body had been cleaned up the rest of the men decided they would eat in the kitchen since Nicholas and I occupied the dining room. I knew he would grill me on why I just did what I did but deep down he already knew the answer so it was pointless for him to ask me the question.

"You're right," he said after he had taken a few bites of his dinner. "I did underestimate you...and you are not who you were before...who you used to be. You're not the same. I can see that now."

I sat quietly – continuing to eat my meal and deciding not to participate in his discussion. I had nothing to say. I had a lot of anger in me – especially today. I felt like a loose cannon. And that Raphael's death would be only the first of many actions to come in the future. I was losing control – self-control and I could feel it. There was no telling who else I would hurt – who else I would kill.

For the first time in my life, I wasn't afraid of dying. My child was alive and she was living with someone who would protect her, always. I knew at any moment one of the men could blow their top over the whole situation. I could almost picture them barging in here just to kill me themself – depending on how much they actually liked Raphael. But I think it was in my favor that a lot of the men saw him as a threat and did not like him as a person.

"I'm going to put Gesella down for her nap," Nario said.

"Thank you, Nario, and when she wakes up Abriana will give her a bath and get her ready for bedtime."

Fast Forward:

For the next hour or so Nicholas and I ate in silence. I could see out of my peripheral vision that he kept shooting glances over at me. Waiting to see if I would look up at him, speak to him, or possibly stab him next. I gave him nothing.

I could hear different conversations making their way in and out of the kitchen. I could feel them staring at us – staring at me – to see if I kept Nicholas alive. I wasn't dumb enough to try to kill him again in a house full of his own men. They should know me better than that. And so should he.

After another half an hour I finished the rest of my dinner and carried my plate into the kitchen without so much as looking over at Nicholas. To my excitement, no one was occupying the space which made it easier for me to slip in and out unnoticed. When I reemerged, I noticed Nicholas was on his last few bites.

"I'm heading up to give Gesella a bath before bed," I said monotoned.

"Don't wake her if she's asleep," he commanded.

Trying to hide my disappointment I responded with, "Fine."

Before finishing my climb up the stairs to the second level I could hear something come crashing down to the floor followed by Gesella screaming. I ran faster than I knew I could – bursting through her door without hesitation. Once inside I found her room to be a wreck. Objects were thrown, and even one of her dressers lay face down on the floor – which I had come to realize may have been the cause for the loud noise I had heard merely seconds before.

Searching under the bed and inside the closet, I found her nowhere until I heard yelling coming from outside the window. At this point, Nicholas was by my side trying desperately to gain my attention and question me about what was happening. Again, the yelling continued and it was only then that Nicholas and I headed to the window.

To our horror, a man was running away from the house carrying our little Gesella over his shoulder. He seemed to be wearing a black t-shirt and because of that, I could make out a large tattoo covering the span of his arm. Off in the distance, I could see her faintly reaching up towards the window at us. She continued to scream with fright, not understanding what was happening. I banged on the window – pounded on it with both fists, screaming her name, screaming for him to stop. At this time most of the men were either piling in the bedroom or standing around the door.

"THE BUTLER STAIRCASE!" Nicholas screamed at the top of his lungs as he took off running.

Many of the men followed him without question and those that stayed behind asked what was going on. It was only then that I realized that was how the kidnapper had gotten away so quickly. He had gotten out of the house like it was nothing. He had known the butler staircase was a back way out of here. And how it would lead him to the kitchen and out the patio door, making it the nearest escape. And with everyone swarming upstairs in the opposite direction there would be no way of catching him. At the time the plan seemed flawless.

It was all I could do but stand at the window and watch as Nicholas sprinted in the direction of the kidnapper. My chest was filled with so much pressure I was certain I would have a heart attack. My knees became numb enough that I found myself slumping onto the window seat. I laid my forehead against the glass just to feel the cold, thinking that would help to calm me.

In my head and my heart, I knew. As a mother – although I didn't want to admit it – I feared she was gone forever and that was the last time I would ever see her. A terribly painful memory forever scorched into my brain.

All that lingered was the remaining question – who would take our daughter in the middle of the night? I patiently waited for what seemed like hours for Nicholas's return. It seemed to be all that I could do. I watched intensely out the window – waiting to see him walking through the yard carrying her in his arms – consoling her, protecting her. But all I saw was darkness. I was surrounded by it.

What karma is this and who is it for? She didn't deserve this – she's a child. And I had just gotten her back. It was all so unfair.

"Come downstairs Abriana," Nario whispered in my ear as he wrapped his arms around the outside of mine and rubbed them softly. "I made a nice pot of coffee – steaming hot. Maybe it will help to warm you up a little bit while we wait."

"Will it warm my insides, Nario? Everything in me is cold at the moment. My body, my heart, it would appear that even my blood has run cold." With that, he guided me silently down the main staircase and into the living room. After sitting me down on the couch, he retrieved a cup of coffee for the both of us.

The few men that did not follow sat in silence occupying various seats spread around the room. Most of them hung their heads with sadness and none of us chose to make eye contact with each other. Now the only sound we would listen to would be the ticking of the clock until any news came.

Chapter XXV

Revenge

Nicholas emerged what seemed like hours later. From his demeanor, I knew it to be bad news. He spoke not one word to any of us as he came in and sat down on the couch beside me. The moment he began to cry was when I knew that what I worried about the most came true. They were unable to catch up to them.

I could feel the lump in my throat make its whereabouts known. It was hard to breathe, hard to swallow, hard to comprehend.

"Who would do something like this?" I finally asked.

With his body still bent between his knees he said, "I think I have a hunch."

"Well don't just keep it to yourself! Share with the group!" I snipped at him in anger.

"Do you remember the family from the deal that went sour years ago?" he asked with a soft mumble. "If you can recall this was before we moved to the manor."

Confused it took me a minute to think back to what he was talking about before I realized. "Yes, how could I forget…when you got shot. I just remember how scared I was when the fever fell upon you."

He laughed at that, chuckling at my recollection. "And do you remember the watcher incident?"

That bad feeling crept over me again. The chills ran up and down until I was sure they covered my whole body. "You mean back when you were pretending to be someone you weren't. Back when you were living under another identity – your alias Gabriele Giuliano. Back when you and your men beat the watcher to death – that incident? Yes, how could I forget that either."

"The watcher was more than just his title. He was the youngest son of a powerful Don – one that had turned down our invitation for the wedding. I believe that this is him seeking revenge. A child for a child."

I couldn't comprehend what I was hearing. This nightmare of his past creeping up to punish us again – but not just him or me, it was our child who was now in the line of fire. *My child.*

"For goodness sakes Nicholas she's just a baby! She's a little girl!"

When he said nothing in response, I fell quiet. I could almost hear his mind formulating a plan. I could smell the burning smoke rolling out from his ears. He wouldn't look at me – probably because he could feel me staring him down with anger. I could kill him. Right here, right now – I wanted to kill him.

"I recognized the tattoo. It was the same one the watcher had. It's a certain family that wears this symbol. That's how I know for certain."

After a moment of silence, I broke down. "Have you ever seen a dying rose? Oh, how silly of me, why of course you have. You've choked too many of them out, I'm sure. Starved them of light, deprived them of water, stole their air. Well, you see when a rose begins to die, you'll first notice the drooping of the head, followed by the darkening of the stem until finally the once vibrantly red petals turn black and begin to fall off – one by one. Until it's nothing but a rotted stem."

"Abriana…I'm afraid I don't underst–"

"I am the rose. I am the rose and you are killing me – yet again. I'm dying because of you. And yet you do nothing because you can do nothing. How is it that you always find a way to destroy me? How can you simply take away everything I have ever loved? She trusted you…and you let her down. You let me down…again."

I couldn't control my tears of pain. I could feel my agony fill the room as the rest of the group began to depressingly make their way out to give us privacy.

"I swear to you – I will do everything in my power to get her back."

Swiftly I rose to my feet to face him. I hovered over him for mere seconds – just long enough for his eyes to reach mine – before striking him across the face with the hardest slap I had ever dealt. "Then what are you still doing sitting here?" I covered my mouth with the back of my hand after I finished screaming and began to cry again – leaving him alone in the room.

When I reached the top of the stairs, I heard Nicholas call out my name – it seemed to take all of the energy left in me to turn and face him. He stood at the bottom of the stairs clenching the banister so tightly that his knuckles appeared ghostly white.

"I *will* get her back, no matter what it takes." Even between clenched teeth, he was so certain of himself, so confident that he would find her and this nightmare would come to an end.

"If you come home without her – I will kill you," I said with no mercy.

"I know you will and I'll willingly let you," he said before turning his back on me and leaving through the front door.

About the author

Christina Casino loves writing novels almost as much as she loves the adrenaline rush of rollercoaster rides. She likes to think of her novels like soft-serve ice cream cones – layers upon layers of swirls and twirls.

Allow her to take you through this ever-growing amusement park of twisted fiction.

You may have recognized her as the author of the unforgettable suspense-filled romance *Unforeseen* that tested your emotions. Or maybe from *The Queen of Hearts* where she took you down the rabbit hole of a lifetime.

Christina enjoys delivering stories to her audience that throw them directly into the character's shoes, forcing them to see through another's eyes. Feel free to follow the author's adventures via her website
www.christinacasino.com

Afterword

My dearest readers,

I am truly honored that you chose *Foreseen* as your next story to venture through the pages of, thank you so much! I hope that you enjoyed reading it as much as I enjoyed writing it.

And please remember that your voice – your opinion matters! And in saying that I would really appreciate it if you would leave an *honest* review for *Foreseen* wherever you have purchased it from. This way we can continue to spread the word and share this novel with others.

As for myself – you can stay up to date on what is happening in my neck of the woods through my website: www.christinacasino.com

I can't thank you enough for everything.

Christina Casino

Additional Author Titles

- ♥ ***Unforeseen*** *– Romantic Suspense /*
  Crime Thriller
- ♥ ***The Queen of Hearts*** *– Fantasy*

Acknowledgments

MANY THANKS FOR YOUR SUPPORT

I just wanted to dedicate this page to all the readers who took the time to purchase and read my novels. As a new author taking her first steps in the writing world – this meant the world to me and I only thought it was right that I give you a shoutout to show how much I appreciated it!

- ♥ Jane
- ♥ Beth
- ♥ Donna
- ♥ Steelmaker
- ♥ All those in the US
- ♥ All those in the UK
- ♥ All those in Australia
- ♥ All those in Brazil
- ♥ All those in Canada
- ♥ All those in Germany
- ♥ All those in India
- ♥ All those in Japan